THE
BLOOD
HOTEL

DESCENT OF THE VILE BOOK 2

CHERYL PEÑA

World Castle Publishing, LLC
Pensacola, Florida
Copyright © Cheryl Peña 2023
Hardback ISBN: 9798390858950
Paperback ISBN: 9781960076502
eBook ISBN: 9781960076519
First Edition World Castle Publishing, LLC, May 1, 2023
http://www.worldcastlepublishing.com
Licensing Notes
Cover: Cheryl Peña
Editor: Karen Fuller

For my mother, Charlotte Peña.
To the best mom I could ever hope to have, thank you for
everything.

CHAPTER ONE

Jackson Riley's breathing became labored even as he saw the bright light soar low in the sky above them. He jogged down the stretch of beach in front of the house he had reclaimed with Nadine Dardenne, who ran along beside him. The stars reflected on the ocean to his left, and he couldn't help but watch the waves roll in toward him, the foam almost glowing in the moonlight. It had been at least five years since Nadine and he had last seen the cyborgs (or whatever they actually were), which had destroyed the world as they knew it. Now, everything was primitive and quiet. Jackson missed his former job as a freelance photographer, his life now full of gardening plots, home repair, and other physical labor. But he had survived, whereas most of the world had not. That was something he could not ignore. He knew he should count himself lucky, but the new world was difficult and dangerous. There were still roving gangs who stole from others for supplies instead of foraging like everyone else. Jackson and Nadine usually carried weapons everywhere they went, although, at that moment, they were unarmed.

But the streak of light had caught his eye. There were so few lights in the new world that he noticed it immediately. Watching intently, he followed it with his gaze as it descended into a field in the near distance. Was it simply a meteor, or was it something else? He knew he should return to the house for one of his guns, but he was afraid he wouldn't find the location again if he left. Looking at Nadine, he tried to gauge her reaction, but she simply appeared frightened and not curious at all. Perhaps she was right to be scared, but he felt the need to check it out. This stretch of beach belonged to them as much as anything belonged to anyone anymore. That made it their responsibility.

All he had to do was point in the direction the object had fallen, and Nadine nodded, already knowing what he wanted to do. They'd lived together long enough that she knew his moods, and now she knew he was going to go investigate whether she went along or not. That was not a good idea. So, he headed across the dunes, looking over his shoulder and knowing she would follow. Normally, he would have simply asked, but they were near enough that he didn't think it would take long to get there anyway.

They crossed over into the tall grass beyond the beach and then had to be careful in the uneven terrain. Jackson crouched down slightly as if he might be observed by someone, but he didn't chance bringing out a flashlight. Of course, in the new darkened world, everyone everywhere brought a light with them. He peered ahead, seeing a glow in the distance where a few trees had grown past the grassland. But the ridge blocked his view of whatever was causing it, and part of him feared the entire area might be on fire. Nevertheless, he continued walking, closer and closer, hearing Nadine's labored breathing almost as much as his own.

Normally, they both took a quick evening jog on the beach for exercise, although they were both exhausted by the time night fell. This time, it was being dragged out, and his legs felt like lead by the time he approached the site. Fear amplified his perception and visual acuity, and he paused just beyond the ridge to try to slow his breathing again before he peered over to see if there was anything amiss.

In a clearing in the trees lay what was obviously an aircraft of some sort. It didn't have wings per se, rounded and somewhat compact instead. But Jackson knew that no one had technology anymore. Several e-bombs had been set off when the cyborgs had invaded, and nothing worked anywhere. So, this was either not from Earth, or someone had developed a new craft from scratch. The second option seemed incredibly unlikely, given how people were living at near Bronze Age levels everywhere. It would require more research and development than before to build something like this, so he watched some more, his fear rising as he saw what looked like an opening appear in the side.

Someone or something was about to come out. The structure was probably about the size of a medium-sized biplane but taller and not quite as long. Not knowing what to expect, he took Nadine's hand, more to keep her from making a sound than for reassurance himself. But maybe he was more nervous than he realized. Her hand tightened on his, and he saw her crouch down next to him, trying to keep out of sight. He dropped to the ground beside her, waiting. Then, something appeared, something metallic and not human at all. It looked like a polished steel frame with an angular head and glowing red eyes embedded in it. The cyborgs. *No.* It couldn't be. But he still saw their forms every night in his nightmares. He would never forget. And now, they had returned.

———

Hurriedly, Jackson and Nadine made their way back to the house in the dark, nearly running, stumbling in the tall grass. When they reached the front door, he could hardly breathe, and she hadn't fared much better. He collapsed onto the floor, closing the door behind him. Although he desperately wanted to do something to destroy the cyborgs, he didn't know how.

Nadine replaced the crossbar in its slot on the doorframe, then she slid to the floor beside him, defeated.

"What can we do? We can't let them take over again. We can't!" he lamented.

It was obvious that she agreed, but she didn't say a word, unable to speak for a few minutes while she struggled for air. Then, instead of replying, she lay her head onto his shoulder, and he was afraid she would begin to weep. Her boyfriend David had been brutally murdered in front of her when the cyborgs had attacked the first time. Jackson couldn't imagine how traumatizing it must have been, but she had rarely spoken about any of it in the interim. Instead, she seemed to be determined to move on. But it was never that simple, and he knew she would be thinking about David now and all that had happened five years earlier when he'd fled Smithton Lake with her.

"We have to go back," Jackson said finally, still not sure it was a good plan but not knowing what else they could do. They couldn't just allow the cyborgs to do whatever they wanted, could they? They would never be free. It was what he had wanted when he'd decided to fight them years ago. But now they were in danger once again.

Nadine lifted her head and turned to him. "What can we do? How can we fight them? We have nothing!"

"We can't let them gain a foothold here. It would mean starting all over again," he protested, his green eyes imploring her. His brown hair had a few grays by now, but he tried to keep it trimmed regardless. He'd shaved his goatee, though, thinking it was too much maintenance, and it didn't matter anyway. No one was there to care whether he dressed fashionably or not. There weren't any fashions anyway anyway.

Nadine's straight black hair had grown down to her mid-back without frequent efforts to keep it in check. He'd trim it for her occasionally to keep it from tangling, but mostly she let it run free, sometimes tying it back from her face to resist the wind. Now, it was coming lose from the band she'd used, and it clung to her skin where she'd been sweating, although it wasn't hot that day. Her hand brushed a strand of it back, and then she shook her head.

"We have nothing!" she repeated, obviously terrified.

He didn't know how to convince her if he wasn't sure himself. How *were* they supposed to fight the cyborgs? Part of him agreed with her, but there wouldn't be anywhere safe as long as the cyborgs were back. He looked around briefly, noticing the walls of the quaint little cottage they had been repairing with his paintings on the walls. For the past few years, he'd been an artist. They'd fought off a few thieves until he'd put the crossbar on the door, but that was all. He wasn't a military hero. He wasn't anyone. She was right. What did he expect to be able to do?

He sighed, exhausted, tired from both running and from adrenaline loss. "We have guns. That's what we have. We can shoot them the way we did in the dome," he suggested, remembering the dome over Smithton Lake where Nadine had blasted them apart when they'd attacked him. But they had to be the high-capacity weapons. Handguns did nothing. The bullets would only bounce off the cyborgs' metal bodies.

"We have to get in close for that," she argued. "They could kill us."

"They could kill us now. We don't have to go looking for them." Looking into her brown eyes, the tears were already starting to form. He hated to say anything to upset her. But he felt he had to convince her, or he would end up going alone. She'd saved his life several times already. He hated the idea of going by himself.

"Then why go looking for them?" she countered. She stared back, her cheeks now wet with her tears, but he knew by now that she wasn't only afraid or sad. She was angry at him.

His hand reached up to dry her face, but she swatted it away.

"What else can we do? Please tell me," he asked her. His voice was raised slightly, but there was no one around to hear them.

"Run. We run," she replied. "Someone else can kill them this time."

"But *will* they?"

"I don't know!" she shouted. "But you don't know either, so please don't act like we're the only ones who can do this. We aren't."

Biting his lip, he tried to decide if she was right. Maybe he was used to the idea of saving the world because it had been the two of them against the cyborgs several years earlier. But the other survivors had come out of hiding, and surely, he and Nadine weren't the only ones who would fight them this time. Then, another thought occurred to him. Who else had seen the spacecraft land? Who else in that sparsely populated region might even know anyone else was there? What if they left things alone and more and more of the cyborgs arrived without any resistance at all?

"What if no one else saw the ship land?" he asked, his voice near silent as he considered the implications. He didn't want to ask her to go with him. He wouldn't. But she was a much better shot than he was, although he'd been practicing. Her rage against them for what they took from her was such that she had much better focus and timing. If anyone could do what he wanted, it was her. But could he ask her to go with him just because he was afraid? Definitely not.

"Okay. Get some sleep," he told her finally. "We'll think about it and decide what to do later."

"Do you think they know we're here?" she fretted slightly.

He tried to decide the best way to answer. "I think they don't. The lights were out when they passed over."

Standing, she wiped her eyes and walked toward the bedroom, pausing to see that he was following her. He wasn't sure if they were really a couple or just friends who shared a space together. She hadn't said any words of affection to him, but then he hadn't to her either. Five years earlier, she'd quit her studies at a university in Paris to live with David in Smithton Lake. It wasn't as if Jackson felt she considered him a peer. He was quite a bit older than she was, in his mid-forties, whereas he knew she was in her late twenties. He'd had an established career and everything. His only real concern was that she might think of him as more of a father figure, which he hoped wasn't the case. There were too few prospects in the world if that were true.

However, instead of climbing into the bed, she reached into the closet and pulled out her overnight bag, slowly stuffing clothes into it as if she were concentrating as she did so. "What are you doing?" he asked, fearing she was leaving him.

"We can go to bed somewhere far from here. I don't want to wait until they find us."

Quickly, he took her bag away from her and set it on the bed. "What if they find us anyway? We don't know that they won't look."

"You're going whether I go with you or not, aren't you?" she challenged him.

Sheepishly, he looked at the floor, avoiding her gaze.

"Then, we go. But we'll be ready to leave if our efforts fail. Is that acceptable?"

He looked up again, realizing she had a lot more wisdom than he'd ever given her credit for. Bravery was one thing. This was another. He conceded that her plan made more sense. "Okay," he agreed.

———

He'd done his best to maintain the Humvee in the intervening years since he'd acquired it, although they had tried to avoid using it given that there was so little fuel left in the area. In the time they'd lived there, on the other side of the country from Smithton Lake, he had felt little desire to leave. It had felt comfortable and far from the stresses of his old life. It was as happy as he was going to be after the end of the world, he thought. Now, he wished they still had gasoline so that they could drive away and be back by morning. But all of the gas had degraded to the point that it no longer burned cleanly enough to be usable. With the world's population so low and all technology wiped out, there was no way to refine any more fuel. Therefore, he and Nadine had rigged two mountain bikes with small, wheeled trailers behind them for storage. He put his bag behind the bike he used, the one with the green camouflage paint job. Nadine's was red.

Then they both began to pedal away from the small house that had been their home for the past few years. Jackson couldn't help feeling a deep sadness, as if he might not see it for a very long time. But he rode out onto the road, keeping the headlamp on low until they were out of the town and back out in the countryside. Then, he turned out the light, riding only with the aid of the moon as he headed in the direction of the ship they'd seen. Their bikes went off-road at that point, crossing over the soft ground until they reached the bottom of the ridge. Jackson climbed off his bike, waiting for Nadine before heading toward the site where they'd seen the aircraft.

He and Nadine climbed the rise until they reached the top, dropping onto the ground and peeking over to see what was now happening where they had been earlier in the evening. There were several more cyborgs, at least thirty, milling around in the wide clearing and setting up a small beacon of sorts at the center. It was cylindrical and had lights surrounding something in the shape of a cone at the top. That was definitely alarming. Jackson didn't want them to be able to call more of the beings across the Emptiness, as they had called their home. He didn't want them to be able to speak to each other either. Whichever the beacon was for, he knew he and Nadine had to destroy it, but there were definitely far more of the cyborgs present than he had expected. They couldn't do this. They couldn't. They would die.

Looking at Nadine, he knew she had been right, and

he now worried about what they could do to stop the cyborgs from taking over again. Could they do anything at all, or were they doomed from the very start several years earlier? Gesturing toward the beacon, he made a gun sign with his hand, signaling they should shoot at it and destroy it before fleeing. Nadine shook her head, but he removed the assault weapon from over his shoulder and aimed it at the small object on the ground. Several of the cyborgs waved tools around it or attached parts to it, making it hum even louder than before.

"Now," Jackson mouthed soundlessly at Nadine, who reluctantly removed her own weapon and aimed it across the clearing, resting the nose of her weapon along a fallen log and in a notch created by a broken limb for support. She nodded at him and held up one, two, then three fingers. At the conclusion, they both fired simultaneously, striking the beacon and then aiming for as many of the cyborgs as they could destroy. However, as soon as he'd paused, it was obvious that the bullets had no effect whatsoever. The cyborgs had made no move to react and simply continued on as before, the beacon completely intact and glowing as if something were protecting it from harm.

Nadine seemed to notice his reaction, and she stopped firing long enough to see that his expression of horror was probably apt. Nothing. Nothing at all. Quickly, Jackson gathered up his gun, grabbed her hand, and raced away from the ridge. They'd given away their position, and it was to no avail, no avail at all. They reached their bicycles, sliding down the low hill and nearly stumbling onto their knees as they reached the bottom. Then, they hurried to climb onto their bikes, Jackson ready to go as soon as he saw that Nadine had climbed onto hers. They sped away from the site, heading away from the coast, away from their new home, away from everything that had become familiar and safe. He no longer had a home, Jackson realized. Nothing would ever be safe again.

––––––––

"What was that?" Nadine asked as they rode away, heading they knew not where.

"What do you mean?" Jackson tried to clarify.

"Our guns didn't do any damage. Why not?" she demanded as if he had any answers.

"I don't know. There must have been some sort of forcefield over it or something. Nothing we could have done would have destroyed it. We put ourselves at risk, and I should have known better. I should have *known*." He stared ahead at the road, berating himself for his lapse. How stupid was he to think they stood a chance? They had nothing but projectiles. The cyborgs had real technology, things humans could only dream about at that point.

"How could you have guessed that?" she asked.

"Why *shouldn't* I have known they had technology we don't have? You said it yourself. 'We have nothing.'" His voice wasn't even bitter. He had given up. What was the point anymore?

He rode straight ahead, not looking at her. He couldn't stand the thought that she might look at him in anger, or worse…pity. Instead, he closed up, and he didn't even know how far he was going, where he would stop, or *if* he would stop. Maybe he would ride until he collapsed from exhaustion. Maybe he'd be killed just like David, and Nadine would be alone. But for how long? Did she stand a chance by herself? Well, maybe she stood a better chance than he did, he decided. She wasn't as idiotic and impulsive.

Then, he wondered if those were his real flaws after all. He'd never thought of himself as impulsive. Maybe it was simply a reaction to seeing the cyborgs again after so long. Maybe he thought they could defeat them because they'd done it once before. But now, he was facing the possibility that he'd risked Nadine's life for nothing, and he didn't want to be responsible. It was easier to say he was impulsive than dense. Then again, trauma did things to people. He'd seen it with Nadine, and while he'd been struggling to understand her, he had felt it had become easier when they no longer had to fear for their lives. She even had a sense of humor that he had started to appreciate. He felt bad that he had never let her express herself before.

Finally, he had to admit to himself that he was traumatized too. He wasn't immune. He was human, and he was afraid. That had always been difficult for him before, admitting that he had flaws and that he was allowed to feel fear. Now, he didn't want to default into his old patterns just because the threat had returned. He didn't want to take his frustrations out on Nadine and shut her out as he'd done previously. But would she retreat into herself as before, hardly speaking? Probably, if he didn't give her the opportunity to speak out. If he continued the way he was going, she would likely feel it was useless to say anything at all. If he didn't listen to her, what would be the point? And then, she'd probably resent him and everything he represented: the loss of David, the return of the cyborgs, and the loss of her innocence.

"I should have listened to you," he said, although minutes had passed with him pedaling in silence.

She turned to him, but her expression was kind. "We'd still be doing what we are now. It doesn't matter."

"What if they come looking for us?" he asked.

"They would have whether we were right there or not. Our shooting at them wasn't a threat. They're going to do what they came here to do, then they'll probably eliminate everyone who's left. That's everyone, not just us."

"This is, strangely, not comforting me at all." He sighed.

"You asked. I'm just telling you." She turned back to the road, and he feared that he'd offended her.

"So, what do you think we should do? Just go somewhere and hide just like before?"

"Just until we can figure out how to destroy them. Then we'll destroy them. Like before." Her voice was firm, and he smiled at her confidence. It was reassuring.

"What if there are more of them?" he asked suddenly. "What if that wasn't the only ship that landed?"

"Then, we're dead," she replied. That wasn't reassuring at all.

———

CHAPTER
TWO

Their bikes pulled into a parking lot behind a small nondescript hotel. They'd seen so many in the past that it didn't stand out at all. It was one of the hundreds of thousands of plain white buildings they'd seen. Only a non-operational neon sign out front indicated that it was somewhere they hadn't stayed before, as none of those had one. Jackson paused, sitting still a moment, bereft of the life he'd built for himself before he finally slid off the bike. He took his bag and waited for Nadine, who took her own bag out of her trailer and followed him to the back door.

Carefully, he opened it a crack, then shone his flashlight inside to check for other occupants, slowly casting the beam around until he was satisfied that the office was empty. Then, he waved Nadine forward, and they both entered the room, closing the door as silently as possible. Then, Jackson cautiously went into the darkened lobby, somehow looking both modern and ancient in 1980s design, his heart racing at the thought that they might not be alone. Nadine was behind him, her weapon held at the ready, just in case. He led the way around the bottom floor, checking the kitchen and dining room, before they went upstairs to check the guest rooms. Once they were satisfied that the hotel was empty, they hurried downstairs to barricade the doors and windows, pushing the bulky furniture up against the glass, heavy wood and metal around the ground floor.

As it was not summer as before, they were saved from the stifling conditions on their previous run across the country, but the still air was uncomfortable as they didn't dare open any windows. He chose a room at random, and they were lucky that the fire failsafe meant the doors were unlocked without the power on. They closed the door and flipped on the deadbolt, then pushed the table in front of it. The room had peeling yellow-gold wallpaper and avocado green bedspreads like it hadn't been redecorated in decades. Lastly, they pushed one of the mattresses up against the window so that they could use the flashlights without being spotted.

Jackson threw himself back on the second bed, covering his face with his hands and feeling like it was far too soon to be doing this again. He didn't want to. It was distressing that things could change so much and yet go back exactly to what they had been like before. Nadine went to the restroom, closing the door for privacy. Thinking about it himself, he realized he probably needed to refresh himself as well, but he didn't feel like getting up.

When Nadine returned, she had her hair down, and her skin looked slightly wet, as if she'd splashed water on her face. She lay beside him on the bed, mostly because there wasn't another place to lie down. Even the house they'd been sharing had only one bed. He supposed they could get separate rooms, but he was used to her presence by then. He wasn't even sure he could sleep without her there anymore, although they had never been intimate. She had never indicated an interest, and he was afraid that any advances on his part might be taken the wrong way. What if they were only meant to be friends or for him to simply be her protector and guardian (not that he thought he was doing a great job in that regard)?

He could tell she wanted to talk, and instantly he felt himself want to close up. Was it a protective measure? Previously, he'd assumed it was a personality flaw, but perhaps he was much more vulnerable than he'd ever let on. Perhaps, he hid it from himself for so long that he wouldn't have recognized it for what it was anyway. He turned to face her, forcing himself to make an effort, even if she decided to go to sleep and ignore everything that had happened after all. But she didn't. She was looking directly at him.

"Why did you rescue me five years ago?" she asked. The question seemed like it should have been something she'd have wanted to know years earlier, but instead, she was asking now. Did he even remember anymore?

"I didn't think about it," he answered. "I just saw you, and I knew I was scared, so you must be, too. It wasn't something I was consciously thinking about, though. You were in danger."

"You didn't think you were doing it because you didn't want me to die?"

"Of course, I didn't want you to die. But if you were asking if there was more to it than that, there wasn't time for that."

She considered and wiped her eyes. "I'm glad you did. I know I told you 'Thank you,' but that's not it exactly. It could have been almost anyone else. I'm glad it was you."

Surprised, he wasn't sure how to react to her statement. It was the first indication he had that she liked him in any way at all. She'd never expressly said so. "Okay, so of everyone I could have saved that day, I'm glad I rescued you. But you do realize you saved my life on more than one occasion after that. There's no way I can ever express how grateful I am, and I feel completely inadequate after that."

She pursed her lips slightly and then bit her lip. "I

didn't do that to pay you back."

"I know. That's what's so amazing about it," he admitted.

Smiling slightly, she wiped her hair back from her eyes. "I'm glad you think so."

"Why wouldn't I?" he said, laughing quietly.

She shrugged. Then, she pulled the blanket up to her shoulders, almost like a barrier. He couldn't tell if she felt threatened suddenly or if she were just cold. But he slid from the bed and hurried to the bathroom, closing the door and quickly relieving himself before washing his hands and face. He took a hand towel to dry himself before heading back into the bedroom. Nadine's eyes were closed when he returned, and he slid under the blankets, turning onto his side and thinking he should try to get some sleep. Perhaps things would be clearer in the morning.

And then Nadine did something she'd never done before. She snuggled against him, her head leaned onto his shoulder for support. She didn't quite put an arm around him, but it was curled in front of her between them. Overwhelmed with emotion, all he could do was feel that he must protect her. He must do better than before. His hand stroked her cheek lightly before he realized that might be taken as a romantic gesture. She was likely only feeling afraid after the incident earlier in the evening. Instead, he reached down and took her hand, holding onto it and giving it a gentle squeeze before he closed his eyes and tried to go to sleep.

———

When Jackson woke, Nadine was still snuggled into his side, but he'd somehow flopped onto his back so that her arm had draped over his chest in her sleep. It seemed far too intimate, so he gently took her arm and moved it so that he could get out of the bed again. She whimpered slightly, and at first, he thought he might have hurt her, but she turned onto her side and immediately fell asleep again, so perhaps it was simply a nightmare.

He took a shower and took care of some basic hygiene before he went back to the bedroom for breakfast. They had both packed a few foods and other supplies, including water, into their bags, but this time, they couldn't rely on canned goods as most of the foods they'd be able to scavenge would have expired by then. So, he took out a small container that held some tomatoes from their garden, thinking it would do. He had a few cucumbers as well, although he would have preferred some citrus in addition to the others. But he ate one of the tomatoes, using tissues from the bathroom as napkins. The fruit was far too juicy and tart for that early in the morning, he thought. However, simply eating a cucumber by itself wasn't very appealing either. Next time, perhaps he would make a small salad with both of them instead.

He had a bottle with a filter in the nozzle that he filled with boiled water from their stores, just in case the water still wasn't potable. Sipping from it made a loud sucking noise, however, and Nadine finally woke upon hearing it. She sat up and looked around for him, finding herself alone in the bed. Then, she saw the light across the room, and she joined him. She took the container with the tomatoes and ate one herself, trying desperately to keep the juice from dripping down her chin, but it was nearly impossible. Afterward, she wiped her face furiously with a tissue as if the whole endeavor had angered her. But then, she sighed and took a sip of water from Jackson's bottle before she went in search of her own.

"What do you want to do?" he asked her as she found her bottle in her bag and then filled it from their stores before returning to the table.

"I want to go home," she replied, apparently feeling despondent. But she sighed again, then continued, "But I suppose we should keep moving. I don't want to be here when they come looking."

"What if they don't? There's no guarantee they'll find us here, is there? We don't even know how many of them are here," he reminded her.

She shook her head. "Do whatever you want."

"I want your opinion."

"No, you don't. You just want me to agree with you." She crossed her arms and waited.

"Fine. Yes, that's what I want. But I was hoping we both thought the same thing. I'm tired. I'm not as young as you are. I don't have the energy to keep going forever. I don't."

"If you want to wait until we're in danger and then leave, you can do that. I just thought it best to get further away." Her tone was matter of fact, however, and not angry, as if she couldn't bother with it anymore.

He found himself becoming angry in response. However, forcing himself to consider her point of view, he tried to think if the cyborgs might already be looking for survivors. They could be. But they might not. Was it better to be careful, though, or to take a chance and risk being caught? Well, if he thought of it like that, the decision was obvious. Besides, he had to remind himself that she'd saved his life

THE BLOOD HOTEL   25

multiple times. He really should listen to her.

"Fine. We'll leave. I don't want to get caught either," he agreed reluctantly.

"It's still morning. We should be safe enough for now."

"No. We'll leave. We'll get further away if we leave early," he thought aloud. "Pack your things, and we'll get out of here."

Silently, she put the clothes she'd slept in back into her bag. They both put away the food but carried their bags and water bottles down to the lobby, which wasn't really a lobby anymore, the barricades still in place. Heaving a sigh of relief, Jackson peeked out of the peephole on the back door, making sure the coast was still clear before opening the door and practically leaping onto his bike. He thought he saw movement out of the corner of his eye, but he began pedaling right as the mob appeared in front of them. He felt vulnerable without the outer shell of a vehicle to protect him, though. Although some of the people had weapons, they didn't hold any firearms, and Jackson raised his gun, firing into the air to scare them away. They scattered. Then, Jackson rode out of the lot and sped down the street, Nadine right beside him, heading for the highway.

"What if that was enough to let the cyborgs know where we are?" Nadine worried.

"We can't be the only people with guns," Jackson countered. "Besides, we're leaving. We'll be fine." He hoped that was true.

Finding the highway, they sped toward another town, heading west, and realized they were also heading back toward Smithton Lake. They had over a thousand miles to go, of course. They could turn off before then, but the very idea was enough to upset him. Neither of them had any desire to return to that area ever again. There was no doubt he would do whatever he had to do to avoid going back there. Nadine didn't need to see the house where David was murdered again, and he didn't need to relive his first encounter with the cyborgs either.

"What are we going to do?" she asked, possibly wondering if he had a plan or if he was just making it up as he went along.

He wanted to say, "I have no idea," but he didn't think that would be very comforting. So, he actually considered his words and tried his best to get along with her. His usual demeanor could be a bit abrasive, he knew. "I think we should head to the next town, then turn north. I don't know if they expect us to go that way, and I don't want to end up back at Smithton Lake."

Nodding, she didn't comment. Perhaps he'd said something she agreed with. And, in actuality, she agreed with him most of the time. It was only when the cyborgs were involved that they were in conflict. It wasn't that she was hard to get along with, far from it. She was probably one of the most resilient and compassionate people he knew (or had used to know — most of his previous acquaintances were probably dead by now). And she had stuck with him even as he had argued with her, even as he had shot down all of her ideas. She'd hopefully realized that he didn't deal with stress well, and that wasn't his normal personality. If so, she was more perceptive than he was, too.

But did he have any real choice but to like her? She was

his only companion in the last several years, the only person he really knew or spent any time with. For her part, she never made any move to leave and never went off to find someone else. Was it all trauma, though? Would she have been better off with someone else, then? But she had said she was glad it was him that had rescued her. Why? He couldn't imagine that.

"Why did you say you were glad I had rescued you?" he asked her finally, his curiosity getting the better of him.

Her gaze dropped to her handlebars, and she gripped them nervously as if she were afraid to voice her opinion suddenly. But then, she returned her gaze to his face, where he was still mostly trying to watch the road. "Someone else would have tried to coerce me to do something I didn't want to do in return."

The thought disgusted him. "I would hope not. But I think there are more decent people out there than we're aware of. You've just run into a lot of jerks, apparently."

"If you had been a woman, I wouldn't have been as nervous. But you never tried to pressure me, and you still don't. I appreciate that you are patient and that you are giving me time to figure things out."

He would have laughed at that, thinking that five years was still an awfully long time, but he didn't want to accidentally offend her. "Five years is probably enough time to figure out whether you're interested or not. It's fine that you're not. Really."

Apparently puzzled, her eyebrows knitted together as if she didn't know what he meant. "Why would you think I'm not interested?"

"You never said anything. It's fine. I mean it."

"It isn't a lack of interest. I just don't know how to…the idea of anything other than platonic contact is scary after I let myself care for David, and then he died. I guess I don't want to…If I let myself…I don't know how to say how I feel."

He wanted to pull over so that he could look at her and make an attempt to understand her point of view. "I never want you to think I expect anything. I don't. And you don't have to say you're interested just because I asked you about it. Just never mind. I never meant to put you on the spot. That wasn't fair of me."

"If there was going to be someone after David, I would want it to be you. But I'm not sure I'm ready for a relationship. It isn't you. It's just everything I've been through. And you, too. I don't know if you're really ready either, you know?" She looked at him as if he might actually comprehend what she was trying to say.

"Maybe I am. Maybe I'm not. I don't even know."

"See." She grinned.

"I'm trying not to think about it. I don't want to put myself or you in a position where either of us will be uncomfortable. So, just forget I asked. I probably didn't think that through enough before I said anything."

"We're allowed to talk about things. It's okay," she said. "I'd rather we talked about it and knew where we both stood than not talk about it and continue walking on eggshells around each other."

"We weren't doing that, though. Walking on eggshells." He was sure he was blundering along as if he had not a care in the world. He'd already stomped on any eggs and crushed them into tiny fragments under his clumsy feet.

"Maybe not, but you can tell me how you feel just as much as you want me to tell you, you know."

Of course, she had a point. "Okay, but what if I said something you didn't like and then things got awkward. I'd rather they stayed the way they were."

"You don't like me?" she asked. And then he wondered where she got that idea from.

"What? Of course, I like you. What does that even mean?"

Shrugging, she looked away.

"I'm not angry. I'm just confused," he explained.

She turned back to him. "That's not what I meant, and you know it. You can tell me. I'd rather know than not know."

"Maybe you only think you want to know. Maybe if you knew, you'd wish I had never said anything."

"Okay, never mind." She paused her bike, took a sip from her water bottle, and then reached into the basket on the front of her bike for the road atlas that she'd left there for emergencies. It was tattered and worn, some of the pages disintegrating, and the words faded. Flipping to the correct page, she stared at it, and he thought she might have been avoiding him. But then, she pointed excitedly at a squiggly line off the main highway, her voice rising in pitch and her hand emphatically gesturing at the mark. "This road turns off up ahead. We don't have to go into the next town."

"Okay. Just keep an eye out for the turn," he told her, hoping he hadn't offended her with his previous statement.

———

Eventually, they approached the junction, and they pulled

off the highway onto the smaller two-lane road. There was nothing but the turn-off. No structures or buildings lay nearby, and they wondered how far they would have to go before they could stop.

"How far until the next town?" he asked.

She spread her fingers apart on the gauge and then placed them on the line indicating the road. "About ten miles," she replied.

He guessed that would have to do. They might have to go even farther still. Their route would have to be unpredictable, as he didn't even know himself where he wanted to go. Hopefully, the cyborgs couldn't tell, either. Feeling halfway asleep, he watched ahead of him, watching the dotted center lines drift past his bike as he traveled along the road. He'd been hungry for years, he felt, and now was no exception. Their little garden plot had been enough for the two of them, but they had needed to trade for additional supplies, and he wished they had more than just a few fruits and vegetables. He especially wanted something he could eat while riding the bike.

"We'll see what the town looks like, then we'll stop and make lunch," he suggested.

They would have to build a fire to cook anything, however. They hadn't been able to find a stove or grill that was portable enough, or that didn't require fuel they couldn't obtain anymore. Propane had already degraded in the intervening years since the first cyborg attack. Butane hadn't fared any better. Nadine nodded, sipping on her water and looking out at the path ahead.

Past the road, mountains rose on either side, covered

in evergreen trees. The road wound around the sides of cliffs and rose over large hills, previous engineers having cut into the sides of the land masses to clear the way for the pavement. A small lake appeared to their left, a swatch of blue in the endless fields of green. It disappeared once they'd rounded a curve, and then they only saw more trees and a few fallen boulders that had toppled long before onto the road from above. Jackson swerved around them, then continued, unfazed by the state of the highway after so long. Potholes were prevalent, and both of them ignored the many bumps and dips as their bikes struck the uneven concrete.

The road conditions slowed them down, and it was nearly an hour later that they reached the town. Jackson rode down the main street, looking around for anything that looked like a hotel or apartment building. Not seeing anything but stores and rubble on the street on his first pass, he made the next turn to go around the corner and then stopped dead in the road.

"Does that look like one of those spacecrafts to you?" he asked.

Nadine's hands gripped her handlebars tightly, and her eyes had gone wide in fear. "Yes. It can't be. There are more of them. There are more of them!" she nearly panicked.

Quickly, they both made a one hundred eighty degree turn in the road, racing away before they could be spotted. But before they could escape, Jackson saw several of the cyborgs lining the intersection, staring straight at them with their glowing red eyes.

———

CHAPTER THREE

Jackson skidded to a halt. Their bikes jolted as they steered them off-road and onto the grass, then trundled over the ground and away from the intersection. However, the cyborgs ran after them, their metallic legs banging against the concrete and making Nadine scream as she heard them approaching. Jackson tried to speed up, but the ground was too soft, covered in long pine needles and soft soil. The wheels mostly spun uselessly until he slowed, then turned the front wheel at an angle, then gradually pushed on the pedals again. His bike began to speed up, and then it bounded across the uneven ground until it made contact with the street again on the other side. Nadine was right behind him.

A beam of light shot out from behind them, vaporizing a tree in their path, but Jackson didn't slow to thank the cyborgs for accidentally removing an obstacle. He sped back toward the main street, heading back the way they'd come, back toward the ten-mile road they'd crossed from the highway. More of the cyborgs were emerging from the spacecraft, joining the pursuit as their legs pounded the ground in unison as if they were acting as one entity. Somehow, Jackson knew it was the beacon, that it had been successfully set up near his home. This spacecraft had only newly arrived, being called from across the Emptiness and then somehow landing in Jackson and Nadine's path once again. How many more were there?

He didn't stop to ponder their bad luck. Instead, both of them pedaled hard and headed toward the highway, several miles away still, and he only wished he'd been able to eat something before they had to leave the town. Trying to put as much distance as possible between them and the cyborgs, he wasn't even trying to be careful. He went as fast as his bike would take him.

———

"Where did that light come from?" Jackson asked as they finally put some distance between them and their pursuers. "I didn't see a weapon."

"It came from its hand," Nadine cried. "Its *hand*."

He tried to calm himself, tried to think rationally and make sense of what was happening. How were they again finding the cyborgs? How could anyone explain it? Were they just that unlucky? "So, they don't need separate weapons?" he thought aloud, still furiously trying to work out the puzzle.

She didn't seem sure he wanted her to answer, so she just sat there, her hands shaking as she tried to drink from her water bottle. Then, she said, "Where can we go that they won't find us?"

"Did they find us, or did we find them this time? The ship was already there when we saw it."

"It doesn't matter. They were there." She took a few shaky breaths and set the bottle back in the cup holder.

"Okay, I'm just trying to figure out what's happening. How many ships came across, do you think? A lot? Or only a few? If it was only a few, then it would be more unusual to have run into them twice. If they sent a lot, then maybe we just can't avoid them. What are we going to do, though? We need to find somewhere to hide for a while, or else we need to figure out if there is somewhere they won't go. I don't want to do this again."

"You wanted to shoot that beacon," she reminded him.

"That was when I thought that's all we needed to do to stop them forever. I don't want to be running anymore. That's different."

Accepting his comment, she leaned back in her seat and closed her eyes, a single tear making its way down her cheek before her hand brushed it away. Perhaps she felt the same as he did. Perhaps she was tired of not having any place of her own. "I don't want to do this either," she told him.

"We'll figure something out, won't we?" he wanted to know.

And she seemed skeptical, but she nodded anyway as if trying to reassure him.

"It was daytime just now," he said suddenly.

"It's still daytime," she commented.

"I know, but the cyborgs were always mostly active at night before. What if something changed? What if they can go out during the day now, too?" he suggested.

She shivered involuntarily. "How will we stop them?" she worried.

"That's my concern," he admitted. They rode further and then saw a gas station up ahead, and he pulled over, hoping there were still some supplies to be gathered. As he parked his bike, he looked back the way they'd come, as if the cyborgs would have run the entire way and caught up to them. He quickly ran inside to gather any supplies that had not already been looted, like some batteries for the flashlights and some first aid supplies. Nadine was watching the door intently as if she hadn't been sure he would return immediately. Packing the items he'd gathered into his bag and then stowing the bag again in his trailer, he looked over at Nadine, who glanced over her shoulder to see if anything was coming up behind them.

"Jackson!" she called suddenly.

He looked up. In the distance, he could definitely see the glint of metal in the sunshine as an entire crowd of cyborgs ran down the road toward them. Abruptly, he climbed onto his bike and then they were speeding away again. "How did they catch up to us?" he said frantically. Looking behind them, he saw the cyborgs drop back, but he wondered how he and Nadine could escape for any length of time if the cyborgs could almost keep up with them as they were only on bicycles.

"What can we do?" Nadine asked. She looked like she might start crying again any moment from fear.

He pushed himself and pedaled as fast as he could, always trying to keep track of Nadine so he wouldn't leave her behind. He wished they had been able to stop in the town. But either way, he needed to get himself and Nadine somewhere safe where they wouldn't be spotted for a long time, especially if they now knew they couldn't outrun the cyborgs. He just hoped it wouldn't be in Smithton Lake.

———

Pulling up to the turn for the highway, Jackson slowed only long enough to get onto the ramp and then sped up again. They both raced toward the next town, worried that the cyborgs could figure out their destination.

"Find me an alternative," he requested urgently. "Find somewhere we can go off of this highway where they might not expect us to go."

Nadine picked up the road atlas again as they paused, the book already turned to the correct page and flipped over the spiral binding. She searched the map, her finger trembling as she traced the line for the highway and finding only a few small towns and not many junctions for other roads. "We've got a way to go to the next one," she told him.

"Great," he commented, not happy. This was what he'd been afraid of when he'd seen the cyborgs again, that they might not be able to get away. It wasn't how he wanted to die.

"What can we do? We can't let them catch us!" she fretted. The countryside was full of old farmland, flat and stretching away to the mountains they were still seeking to leave. There wasn't any way to cut across the fields to get to a junction any quicker. From the map, however, the terrain was so rough that they hoped it would slow down the cyborgs just as it slowed their bikes.

He looked ahead of them on the road, trying to come up with a plan. Nothing seemed to reveal itself, no matter how he wished for it. He looked to Nadine for support, but she was studying the map as if the solution lay there. Maybe it did, maybe it didn't. Where else could they look? What else could they do?

Starting up again, they raced away from the junction. Up ahead, he saw a turn, but it was a private road. Still no good. There would be no escape if they were caught. He kept going, the road stretching out in front of him and almost mocking him. This was his life now. Running. Again. Bitterness filled him as he thought about the cyborgs and everything they had done to ruin his life and everyone else's. He wished he could think of a final solution, but that was nearly impossible without the technology to do so, wasn't it? Humanity had nothing left. The cyborgs had the advantage.

When they reached Buford, the next town, Jackson was

tempted to turn off to take the next exit off the highway, but then he thought that would be too obvious. "This exit or the next one?" he asked Nadine.

She looked at the map again, still looking for the perfect hiding place, as if the map would reveal it. Finally, she shrugged and said, "The next one, I think."

If she thought so, too, he hoped they had a better chance. They rode past the turn off and continued down the highway, feeling exhaustion taking over. Sleep. He needed sleep. But would they be able to stop long enough to rest? It seemed unlikely. Their bikes shot past another small town, but there wasn't a junction at the stop, so they kept going. Further along, he thought he could see a major intersection coming up like another interstate met up with the one they were on. Was that too obvious, too?

Unsure, he assumed they had no choice. It was either that or they stayed where they were, easily exposed and vulnerable. So, they took the exit, thinking they would seek out another turn as soon as they could find one. For some reason, the smaller, less-traveled roads seemed safer, although Jackson wasn't sure why he thought that if they were nearly caught on one of those. However, there were miles and miles of country roads, and he thought there had to be a route the cyborgs hadn't yet discovered.

He wanted to be able to have a real conversation, but he didn't want to be distracted with both of them pedaling as fast as they could. It was dangerous, and he didn't want to cause their demise any more than he wanted the cyborgs to. For her part, Nadine seemed to realize the danger, and she rode silently, only periodically pausing to check the map for options. But he knew it was hard to read it with them riding over the rough road, so she wasn't looking at it as often as she probably wanted to. But she pointed out a junction up ahead, so they took the turn, nearly toppling their bikes over as the ramp came up faster than they had expected. Then, they hurried to disappear amid the foliage to the sides of the road. They were quickly enveloped by towering pine trees, and they both hoped they could slow down. There would likely be more obstacles on this route, too.

To prove them right, a fallen boulder appeared in front of them, and they braked hard to avoid colliding with it. The mountain rose to Jackson's right, and he carefully brought the bike around the left side, the trees the only things between him and a thirty-foot drop. A few inches of road extended beyond the boulder, but even the bike's trailer's tires barely fit in the space. Jackson was concentrating, sweat dripping down the sides of his face as he slowly crept forward to avoid rolling his bike down the mountainside. When he was free, he could barely believe that he was clear, and he looked back to make sure Nadine made it safely through before they resumed hurtling along at their top speed, despite the risk.

The road was in poor condition after so long without repairs, and their bikes roughly bounced around the potholes and dips and bumps. It was exhausting trying to stay on the road, but Jackson saw no movement behind them. He finally paused, pulling his bike behind an empty gas station they found on the route. His legs ached when they arrived, but he decided they needed to eat first. They quickly dug into their bags and ate some of their fresh tomatoes, watching and listening for anything that might be amiss. Then Jackson rode around to the front again, leery of any possible intruders, but he rejoined the road, and then they took off again.

They came up on another junction, and Jackson debated taking the turn, but in the end, he decided against it, thinking to take the next one. They raced past it, their bikes a blur as they sped along the road. Sometimes they encountered more obstacles, like a sinkhole that had destroyed part of the pavement. Luckily, the mountain wasn't as steep there, so their bikes could go around it. The mountain bikes did so fairly easily, even if they were jolted around as their wheels went over the uneven ground.

When they reached Dumont, another small town, darkness had started to descend. The headlamps barely illuminated the buildings, and they strained their eyes to see. Jackson rode with Nadine down the main street, turning off the county road and heading where he hoped there would be a place to stop for the night. A white building caught their eyes, a small three-story building that looked like it might have been apartments. He rode into the small parking lot for residents, hoping they could gain entry. The leasing office was on the first floor, and Jackson took his flashlight inside with Nadine behind him, covering him with her weapon. The keys were in a box attached to the wall behind a door that probably should have been locked. The inhabitants must have left in a hurry, he thought. He took one of the keys, noting which apartment it was for and making sure it was upstairs before they left to find the right unit.

Once they went up the stairs, he found the apartment they were looking for. It was small. A one-bedroom with mission-style wood furnishings and a bulky leather sofa. He opened the door, going slowly so that Nadine could keep up with him. They searched the space, finding no one. Then, they barricaded the door and the small window. There was no balcony, so that was a relief. One fewer thing to worry about. They were disappointed that the unit only had electric appliances, so they weren't able to cook anything as if even the natural gas might have still been in the lines and not been degraded. So, they ate more of their stores raw, as before. Then, they found the bedroom and fell upon the bed as if they hadn't seen one in years.

Jackson thought he would fall asleep immediately, but he lay awake worrying. Perhaps Nadine was worried, too, because she tossed and turned and wouldn't lie still. Finally, he flopped onto his back and heaved a sigh, frustrated that he couldn't get himself to do what he most needed to do. His body fought off sleep as if it were poison. Sometimes, he would feel its pull, but then he resisted, even seeing the dream begin before his eyes. But he would wake, and he'd see the room around him looking completely ordinary. Part of him was afraid that if he slept, he would have nightmares, so perhaps that was what he was trying to avoid.

Nadine was facing him again, as always, close but not really touching. He wanted to talk to her about his concerns, but he feared that would stress her out more than before. However, he knew it wasn't healthy to keep things to himself. He couldn't tell if her eyes were open or closed in the blackness, but he hoped she was awake. Then again, what could he say? He was worried they would die. Well, she was probably already worried about the same thing. Closing his eyes again, he hoped to fall asleep. He needed to recharge before morning, when they would likely be fleeing again.

But how could they stop the cyborgs? They couldn't let them get away with what they were doing, likely trying to eliminate the life on this planet to favor themselves. Jackson and Nadine had stopped them with e-bombs before, but what if he couldn't construct one on his own? He knew nothing about it, and he didn't want to do something pointless, either. What if the cyborgs were more scattered this time? What if it was nearly impossible to kill them? The last time, there were thousands of cyborgs in one place. How many were here now? Enough to target them with a blast, or should he wait to see what they were going to do first?

"What is that?" Nadine asked suddenly.

He couldn't see anything in the blackness of the room. "I don't see anything," he told her.

"No. That noise," she clarified.

But he couldn't hear anything, only crickets outside in the grass. "I don't —" And then it became clear to him. It was a rhythmic pounding, like metal striking a solid surface far off in the distance. But it seemed to be getting louder, as if whatever was causing it was coming closer. He knew it was the cyborgs. What else could it be?

Nadine whimpered, and he took her in his arms and held her tightly. She was shaking, and he couldn't calm her. What could he do to make sure they were safe? The noise became louder and louder. It seemed to be everywhere, surrounding the town. That meant there were more cyborgs than he had seen in that one spacecraft. There were *lots* more. He felt his own breathing quicken, and then his hands shook as he held onto Nadine. Would the cyborgs recognize their bikes parked outside? Would they come looking for them? Yes. Of course, they would. They had said it before. "No human was insignificant." He'd taken it as motivation at the time, but the cyborgs would kill the two of them to make room for who knew how many *more* of the cyborgs.

"We're going to be fine," he whispered to Nadine as the cyborgs walked outside the building now, so close that he was sure they would be found. The pounding noise grew louder down below their window. He could hear something else, like a humming noise in the background. They were looking for survivors. He didn't know how he knew. But the dome over Smithton Lake had hummed, and he had been sure it was some sort of location technology. What if this was the same?

"Don't move," he said into Nadine's ear, trying to move as little as possible. She would have acknowledged, but she held still and silent, not saying a word.

He could feel his breathing become more ragged as he pictured themselves being torn apart. The cyborgs wouldn't wait until they were dead, either. Fear caused his adrenaline to surge, and then he was sweating again as if he'd run a marathon. What if the cyborgs could sense heat? What if they could see him and Nadine huddled together, terrified in the darkness? His arms were tired, but he couldn't have released her if he'd wanted to. He could barely move in his terror. She was barely breathing, only small, rapid gasps escaping her lips, and he was afraid she would hyperventilate.

However, his usual words of encouragement couldn't be expressed. He had to hope she could tell he wouldn't leave her, that he would stay with her until it was over, however, it ended. The banging outside seemed to concentrate around the town as if the cyborgs knew where they were hiding. Jackson could hear them, not only around the apartments but everywhere. Surely, the cyborgs could figure it out. And then, slowly, the sounds began to diminish. At first, he thought he was imagining it, that it was only wishful thinking. But then, the sounds moved away and eventually grew silent as if the cyborgs were moving on. Had they not found what they were looking for? Or were they simply waiting for a better time? He didn't care. He was alive.

————

CHAPTER
FOUR

Wanting to release Nadine, he found he couldn't voice how he was feeling in words. Instead, he simply held her tighter than before and leaned his forehead down onto hers, glad she was still there with him. Then, her arms wrapped around him, and she squeezed until she was against him, her entire body safely shrouded by his. She wept quietly, and he nearly broke down himself, unsure the ordeal was really over. Of course, the cyborgs could come back. They *would* come back. But for now, he and Nadine were both alive.

Eventually, he relaxed his arms. He couldn't see her, but he knew she was still there, still cuddled up against him. His hand stroked her hair, in an effort to comfort her, but then, he wasn't sure how she would accept the small gesture of affection. He almost apologized, but then he felt her lips on his, soft and warm as if she were afraid this was her last night on Earth. Until that moment, he had no idea that he was attracted to her, no idea that she felt anything for him, either. He pressed his lips to hers, his fingers entwining in her hair. Slowly, he moved his lips down her neck, and then he just froze. He couldn't just allow himself to get carried away with passion. What if she was only trying to thank him? Her kiss wasn't necessarily a proposition. He didn't want to misjudge her intent any more than he wanted to give her the wrong idea about himself, either.

Her hand found his in the darkness, and she held it. Then he felt gentle kisses along his fingers and then his palm. She took his hand and placed it under her bra and on her breast before she took her fingers and began unbuttoning his shirt. Her desire couldn't have been more obvious at that point, but would she feel the same if they hadn't just survived the cyborgs stalking?

"Are you sure?" he asked, thinking that if they acted on any impulses she would regret it later. And he didn't want to be a regret.

"Yes," she whispered. She had almost removed his shirt, her fingers caressing his chest.

"What if you change your mind after? We can't take it back," he reminded her.

"I don't want to take it back," she said, her lips now on his skin, and he could feel the air on her moist kisses, the chill in the air making him desire her more.

Then, he found the bottom of her blouse and pulled it up and over her head. Although he couldn't see her, he could sense her body in the darkness, and he carefully but urgently found her breasts and slid his hands over them, trying not to hurt her. She moaned in response to his caresses, and he felt an overwhelming sense of exhilaration at her pleasure. They may not have any more chances than that night, but to him, it was worth it just to bring her a few moments of happiness.

———————

It was nearly impossible to tell if it were morning or still the middle of the night. As they'd blocked off the window, hardly any light came in from outside, and all he knew was that Nadine was still against him, naked and vulnerable. Hoping she still felt the same way as the night before, he pushed a strand of hair back from her face and kissed her gently, feeling her stir, and then he could tell that she was smiling from the feel of her lips against his.

"Good morning," he told her.

"Good morning," she responded, her voice shy, as if

she might be afraid of what he thought of her.

He didn't know why it had taken a near-death experience for him to finally bond with her, but he only knew he didn't want her to be afraid. "Are you okay?" he asked.

"I think so. Are you?" she replied.

Was he? He wasn't sure either. "Yeah," he said anyway. His thumb caressed her cheek then he felt her hand on his back as if she were tracing his muscles with her fingers. Suddenly, he felt his desire rekindle. His lips finding her breast, he felt her nails dig into his skin, and she gasped before he abruptly stopped and oh so reluctantly realized they should probably get out of that apartment and go somewhere far away. Although it was tempting to stay there with her, he also knew they weren't safe. They'd already almost been found.

"Don't stop," she whimpered, but he had to. He sat up, taking her hand and giving it a quick peck in apology before he reclaimed his clothes.

"We should get out of here." He rubbed his eyes from lack of sleep. "We don't want to stay here another night. Do you know what time it is?"

Groaning slightly, she sat up, but she found her clothes and then stood to peek out the window. As she pulled back part of the barricade, he could see the sunlight illuminate her silhouette, and he knew it was already getting late. "It looks like it might be mid-morning," came her answer.

He sighed, wishing they didn't have to worry about the cyborgs anymore. He would have liked to enjoy a few more moments of intimacy, getting to know her as he hadn't known her previously. But he knew that was a dream, something he couldn't indulge in right now. "We should get going, then."

His voice expressed just how hesitant he was to move from that room. But he got dressed, hearing Nadine's movements and knowing she was doing the same.

Then, he found the food stores in their bags and a knife in the kitchen, taking a few moments to chop a tomato and cucumber together to make a salad for both of them. They ate quickly before he took up the flashlight again, and she had her automatic rifle slung over her shoulder. He checked out the peephole to make sure nothing was waiting for them outside the door, then they opened it and warily made their way down to the first floor, then out to the parking lot where they'd left their bikes. The bikes still looked to be undiscovered and undamaged, so they put their bags in their individual trailers before climbing back into the seats.

Jackson almost expected a line of cyborgs to be waiting for them, although he didn't know why. But he didn't see anything amiss. "Which way?" he asked, looking to Nadine with the map.

"We can go left at the junction up ahead," she answered, showing him the picture and pointing to the symbol she had mentioned.

He nodded, then they pulled out of the lot, almost expecting to be overrun by cyborgs in hiding. But there was nothing. The road led to a junction about a mile away, where they turned left and headed north. The mountains grew steeper, and the trees covering them denser as they traveled farther and farther from the town. Soon they could hardly see anything but the towering pines on either side of the road, the branches blotting out most of the view beyond.

Reducing his speed due to the lower visibility, he

became nervous that something might be waiting for them up ahead or that the cyborgs would come up from behind them and catch up to them. Even so, he realized he didn't even know where the cyborgs were. Had they moved on to the surrounding areas to search, or were there more of them still coming? His anxiety increased as they crested a rise, and he couldn't see over it to the other side. However, when they descended the hill, he could see that there were just more trees, the sunlight slanting through them to create long shadows across the road.

When they next came upon a town, it was obvious that it had been deserted for a long time. The buildings were more dilapidated than most of the others they had seen, and when he looked for a place to stop, the windows were all shattered, and the floors were ripped up.

"How far to another town?" he asked Nadine.

She analyzed the map and showed him. The next stop was a large city called Seven Springs. He hoped that meant there were more places to stop and more supplies to be gathered. It looked to be no more than another few miles away, so he thought they should have enough energy to make it that far, especially if there might be a hotel or apartment building on the outskirts of the city. Parts of the road had nearly washed out due to weather, however, and the going was slow. He thought it might take another thirty minutes to get there, but it was nearly an hour before he saw any signs that they were nearing the city limits.

Seeing a convenience store with a rusty sign hanging over it, he pulled into the parking lot and then froze, his blood running cold at the sight of a cyborg standing in front of the store. He was afraid to move, afraid to breathe. The mechanical being didn't seem to notice him, however. In fact, looking closer, he didn't see that the red eyes were alight or that it had even moved at all since he'd pulled into the lot. Cautiously, he let out his breath, then dropped to the ground beside his bike, his shoes crunching on the loose gravel as he approached the metal form against the wall. It didn't move at all, but that didn't mean it wasn't dangerous.

His hand reached out as he neared it, and he waited for the thing to clamp onto his arm as one had done once before years ago. It still didn't move. The eyes were dead, and he thought it looked like some of the pieces were missing as he looked closer. He touched it, and nothing happened. Then, he gave it a gentle shove, and the remains toppled over onto the pavement. Well, that was a relief, he thought. But should he keep the cyborg as a way to determine any weaknesses, or was it too dangerous to attempt? He wasn't sure, but he didn't exactly want to ride across the country with a cyborg corpse in the trailer behind his bike anyway.

Nadine stepped off her bike after him, slowly approaching and then putting her hand on his shoulder. "Let's go before it wakes up," she suggested.

"I don't think it's going to. Parts of it are missing," he replied.

"How do we know that the parts it needs to function are the parts that are missing?" she asked.

He thought she might be right, but he didn't want to miss the opportunity. He wanted to rest a moment while he tried to decide what to do. His legs burned, and he felt exhausted as he hadn't ridden his bike that much in all the years he'd had it. But he couldn't fathom how to fit the thing in the trailer or how he would be able to tow its weight with only his own strength to do so.

"What if we took that with us and tried to see if they have any weaknesses?" He gestured toward the cyborg on the ground.

She seemed to shiver. "I don't want it near us. It might kill us."

"What if we don't get an opportunity like this again?" he asked.

She nodded. "Exactly. What if we don't get another opportunity because we're dead?"

Was she trying to make a joke, he wondered? Maybe not. But he felt it was their best chance to survive. "I still think we should bring it. We can...I don't know. We can see if there is anything that can kill them besides an EMP."

"We're not scientists," she reminded him.

"Maybe not. But what if there aren't any scientists anywhere?"

She seemed to consider what he'd said, and she paced back and forth in the small space in front of the store. "Do you think you can do this? Really? I mean, what do you plan to do with it first?"

He shrugged, realizing that he wasn't exactly sure. "How about we find a library and research possible experiments?"

"If you think it's worth the risk, you can bring it. But dump it at the first sign of danger, please."

"Trust me. That was the plan," he agreed.

"Okay. But we'll also need a place with equipment to

test it," she said.

He grumbled slightly, but he conceded her point. "We'll find something. This is a big city."

"You don't think there will be lots of cyborgs there like before?" she worried.

"Actually, I'm not sure. They're not acting like they were before. But they might be. We just have to look. And be careful."

"What if there aren't any more laboratories?" she asked.

"There might not be, but we'll worry about that if we encounter that problem. Until then, we can try to bring the cyborg and find a place to test it for vulnerabilities. If we can't find anything, we'll leave it behind. Is that acceptable?"

Reluctantly, she nodded, staring at her feet on the ground.

"I know you don't like this. I will remember what you said," he told her.

"It might be too late for that."

———

They both maneuvered the metal form of the cyborg into Jackson's trailer. It seemed to weigh a ton, but they struggled until they managed to get it jumbled into the space. Jackson was sure he must have slipped a few discs in his back doing so, but they rode away and toward the inner city, where towering skyscrapers were already crumbling and no longer the pinnacles of civilization that they once were.

Everywhere the streets were empty and full of rubble. The majority of survivors had clustered in smaller towns where they could more easily access the farms on the outskirts.

There were a few who were still nomadic, but those were the minority. It was easier to settle and grow food than to scavenge for supplies. However, humanity had been nearly wiped out by the cyborgs and by rampant disease afterward, where there were no longer any cures or vaccines without the technology to make them. The large cities were concrete and glass wastelands.

The sight of the shells of old vehicles and the deserted buildings were unsettling, but they were used to it by now. Everywhere else looked the same. Some of the road signs had collapsed onto the highway, but their bikes were steady enough to ride over them when needed. At other times, they struggled to read the words on the walls of some of the buildings, the lettering already coming off and difficult to read. Everywhere, weeds had started to grow between cracks and were helping to destroy what was left of the structures. In some places, the weeds had caused walls to crack and pavement to crumble.

Eventually, Jackson deciphered the words "metropolitan library" amid the jumble of greenery in front of a building the size of a city block, five stories tall, and sporting the remains of a beige colored paint job from years before. The next block over held the parking garage, and Jackson hoped that would hide their bikes from the view of any cyborgs that might be present. He pulled into the darkened garage and circled until he came to the walkway across from the front door. Leaving their guest in his trailer, they crossed to the front door, which surprisingly swung open at a slight push from Jackson.

Using their flashlights, they searched the ground floor

for signs indicating the layout or for any sort of floor plan. Perhaps the papers at the front desk had depicted maps once, but the ink had faded in the years since they had been printed, and they were illegible. Jackson walked through the building until he came to the elevators, which were inoperable, but there was a plexiglass panel bolted to the wall, which showed their current location relative to the rest of the building. Happily, he noted where the nonfiction science books were likely to be located, and then he led Nadine up to the fourth floor via the emergency stairwell.

The grayish-pink carpet had molded in places, and some of the tiles were coming up, revealing concrete beneath them. Jackson almost tripped over one before he'd found that out, but then he held the flashlight lower, making sure there weren't any items on the floor that might prove hazardous. Even a small cut or abrasion might prove fatal due to a possible infection, or at least it might make one of them sick for several days. They couldn't afford to be indisposed for any length of time, as they weren't sure what would happen. So, he wound around the stacks of books and near ceiling-high shelves, hoping to find what he needed. Surely, the cyborgs had weaknesses. He just had to do the right experiment to determine what they were.

Some of the signs on the shelves had come off and were lying on the floor where they had fallen. He carefully picked them up and read off the numbers until he found the section he was looking for. Then, both he and Nadine scanned the titles for anything that sounded promising. A few times, Jackson removed a book from the shelf, only to decide that it wasn't useful, and he would place it back as if another patron would come one day to check it out later. A few of the books were so badly damaged by humidity that the pages stuck together. The chances of finding what he needed were slim, and he started to realize that his idea was probably completely unrealistic, and they wouldn't get it to work. Most of the books came apart when he tried to open them, the spines separating from the pages as he cracked them to view the table of contents.

"This is crazy," he commented.

"Yeah. I'm not sure we're going to find anything," Nadine agreed. She tried to put a book back on the shelf, but it slipped from her fingers and then made a loud clapping noise as it struck the floor.

Jackson froze, almost sure he'd heard something in response, something other than the book landing on the damaged carpet tiles. Nadine reached down to pick up the book, but he held out a hand to stop her. "Shh."

She stood and listened while he started to walk back the way they'd come, back toward the stairs. Then, he heard it again. A whispering. There were others here, he thought, alarmed. But why? A library didn't contain anything of value except knowledge, and this one was clearly nearing the end of its life. He waved to Nadine to follow him, and they tiptoed across to the stairs, both trying to determine where the sounds were coming from.

But then, something out the window caught his eye. Was it a light? No. It must have been the reflection from his flashlight, he thought. But then, the color was wrong. His light was white, but the light he'd seen was orange. Walking then to the window, he looked out, seeing no sign of anything unusual. But something seemed wrong. He looked down to the street below before the light again caught in the reflection from the building across the street. There *were* cyborgs there. They stood in a cluster around the entrance, where they'd set it ablaze. Black smoke consumed the lobby, the cyborgs standing still amid the orange and yellow flames, waiting.

That was the whisper. It wasn't anyone talking at all. It was the crackle of a fire as it raced through the bottom floors. Even in their current state, the books would burn. *Everything* would burn.

————

CHAPTER FIVE

Smoke began to float close to the ceiling as it slowly penetrated the wide room. Nadine coughed, her eyes flooded with fear. Jackson frantically searched for an escape route, but he knew the elevators wouldn't be operational. He also knew from the reflection that the building entrance was already blocked. What could they do? They crouched down, then peeked into the stairwell, hoping it was far enough from the entrance that it might have escaped the flames. But how would they get out? Surely, any back door would have been blocked, as well.

He tried to remember what he saw on the map by the elevator, but he could only remember where he'd seen the location of the science books in relation to the others. He hadn't been looking for anything else. Changing tactics, they both hurried to the elevators, hoping the map on that floor was still intact. It was difficult to see with the smoke now filling the room, but he could determine that there was a basement with an outlet to the street, where special events took place. Hopefully, the cyborgs had overlooked it. Leading Nadine down the stairs nearby, he wished their footsteps were quieter as they tried to outrun the smoke and not attract any unwanted attention. Their flashlights only illuminated inches ahead of them, the smoke like a solid wall in front of them.

They slowed as they neared floor one, hoping the cyborgs hadn't been staking it out, but they saw no one. However, the smoke was thicker there, and they could hardly breathe. Did that mean the fire was below them, as well? Jackson worried they were stuck there and would die painfully, consumed by the flames. He coughed constantly, unable to stop, but he feared attracting the attention of the cyborgs, letting them know where he and Nadine were at that moment. He thought he could see a flash of orange light on the doors, but he held his shirt over his mouth to aid his breathing as he tried to help Nadine past the obstacle. They squeezed against the far wall, hoping they weren't making matters worse by walking down into an inferno.

Descending further, they found themselves at the bottom, where a large letter B painted on the wall told them they had reached the basement. Jackson feared touching the doorknob even as he cautiously placed his hand against the door to check the temperature. Determining that it wasn't blocked by fire, he used his shirt to reach out and pull the handle down, ducking down as smoke surged in from the open door, the wide space beyond currently awash with the dangerous conflagration, nearly engulfed by flames. Jackson pulled Nadine into the space, still fearing it was a mistake, and they ran toward the door, which hopefully led to the lower level of the parking garage. Holding their shirts up over their heads to protect themselves, they tried to avoid the bits of debris falling from the ceiling. A small cinder caught on Nadine's blouse, however, and Jackson quickly used his bare hands to put it out, desperate to protect her. His hands were only mildly burned in the effort, but it was worth it to him.

When they reached the exit, he pushed on the door, afraid there would be cyborgs surrounding it, but they seemed to have neglected it. He took Nadine's hand, and they ran across to the garage, sprinting up the stairs to the next level, the street level, where they'd parked their bikes, trying not to cough as their lungs got a taste of clean air. Then they both looked across to where the two bikes sat alone in the space. The cyborgs gathered a few hundred feet away. Could they make it? Briefly, Jackson considered leaving everything behind, but they needed their food and the medical supplies he'd managed to bring.

He turned off the flashlight in his hand, trying not to draw any more attention to himself. Taking a few deep breaths to steady his nerves, he finally decided that he should move slowly at first. Inching toward the bike, he made sure Nadine was with him, and they laboriously took one slow step at a time, nearing their bikes at an agonizing pace. He paused briefly to make sure he had not been observed, then continued, Nadine matching his movements and trying to stay out of sight. Eventually, he reached his camouflage-colored bike, and he had to turn his back to mount it. He watched the reflection in the library window nearest him as he silently tried to lift his leg up and over. Nadine was already on hers, waiting.

It must have been too much. The cyborgs turned, and their eyes flared, then a sound almost like an alarm blared out of them. He gave up on caution, climbing into the seat and then pedaling hard to get away from the front of the garage. Remembering how heavy the dead cyborg had been, he knew he couldn't ram them with only a bicycle, but he turned around, heading toward where he'd entered the garage at the back of the structure. Both of them raced around the cross arm at the entrance, then the cyborgs converged on them. Jackson wasn't sure they could escape, but they rode as quickly as they could, still slightly ahead of the cyborgs as they sped away from the library, orange flames licking up the sides of the building. Looking carefully over his shoulder, Jackson saw the cyborgs return to their places, walking through the conflagration as if it didn't exist.

If the cyborgs didn't know before, they now knew Jackson had a camouflage painted bike, and Nadine had a red one. However, they'd found him and Nadine at the library, he didn't know. He only knew he feared staying overnight in the same city as the cyborgs. They raced away from the metropolis, wondering where was safe and what they could do to rid themselves of the cyborgs once and for all. It didn't have to fall on him, but it probably did. The cyborgs seemed to have chosen him as a target in one way or another.

"They can walk through fire?" Nadine asked incredulously. She shivered next to him on her bike, trying to pedal and talk at the same time, and he could tell that she could feel the presence of the one in his trailer more than before. Her eyes flicked in that direction, probably feeling like she wanted to be rid of it. "How can we kill them? They can walk through *fire!*"

"I don't know. Let me think a bit," he countered, still reeling. They weren't out of the city yet, several miles to go before they were out of the area, but he wished they had a laboratory or someplace to test out theories. How else could they destroy beings that, as she had noted, could walk through fire?

"How did they find us?" she continued in her previous vein. "They couldn't have tracked us from the other stop. They didn't find us there."

"I don't know," he repeated. "I need to think about it."

Sighing, she wiped her eyes. "I want them gone for what they did."

"I know. I do, too," he assured her. "I just don't know what to do without being able to do experiments."

"We don't know that a laboratory would have been in working order. Most of the equipment probably runs on electricity," she pointed out.

He paused. "Yeah."

"So, how can we do anything? We can't even determine if they have any weaknesses! If *fire* isn't one of them—"

"I don't know yet. We'll think of something, okay?"

She wiped her eyes, looking more tired than he'd seen her before. The entire incident was taking its toll, and it may have only just started. He had no clue how to end the cyborgs' occupation. No clue at all. They would probably end up running for a while, and he wasn't even sure they could survive if the cyborgs had already managed to track him somehow. What if they were still doing it and would find him wherever he ended up?

Eventually, they were out of the downtown area, heading into the suburbs. He wanted to stop there but knew they probably needed to get farther away. The next town wasn't far enough either. Did they want to continue the way they were going, or did they want to turn off and try to randomize their path a little more? He wasn't sure it mattered. He hadn't known he'd end up in the city, but the cyborgs had figured it out anyway. They'd still found him. Where could he go that they wouldn't expect?

He rode as quickly as he could go, reaching the highway onramp and then speeding along it onto the highway and then toward the countryside. When they had reached the city limits, he wanted to breathe a sigh of relief, but they still had no idea what would happen. Were they any safer between towns, or did it make no difference whatsoever? Back in the mountains, they slowed slightly to be able to navigate the terrain. Sometimes the road wound around the side of a cliff, and he could barely see around the curve to tell if the road had been washed out or if there were any other obstacles. Only his desire to escape kept him going faster than he would have liked to go.

Even worse, as his full concentration was on the ride, he couldn't think about anything else. Would they end up in a trap wherever they decided to stop, or would they have a few hours to think of a plan? He wasn't sure, but he'd wanted to have a few ideas already. Instead, he carefully steered around boulders and potholes that were too deep to go through. Landslides blocked their path a few times, as well. Their bikes could go over them if they weren't very steep, but sometimes they had to find a way around. Unfortunately, it was also time-consuming, and he feared the cyborgs would already be heading toward his unknown resting place.

As they neared sunset, he knew they would have to stop. They didn't want to be out on the roads at night, based on the old pattern, although the cyborgs had now attacked them in full daylight, so he wasn't sure if there was a safer time anymore. They rested a few minutes on the side of the road again before they entered another town called Lowe, a few miles from the interstate they'd been on before. Pulling into a hotel parking lot, Jackson hoped they would have time to rest before fleeing again (which he knew was likely). The hotel was off the main street, with a white stone exterior and a sign outside that read "Inn," as the name had somehow faded with time.

The parking lot was to the rear of the hotel, so he hoped their bikes weren't too visible. They entered through the back door as before, securing the lower floor before going upstairs to search the rooms. They checked each floor for other occupants before reaching the topmost floor, the fifth floor, and choosing a room near the stairs. When they'd locked the door, they pushed one of the mattresses against the blackout curtain for added security, then pushed the table against the door. They didn't even discuss it. They just knew.

Jackson set the flashlight bulb up on the table while he searched his bag for some food. They had preserves in addition to the fresh tomatoes and cucumbers, but he didn't want to eat those until the fresh fruit had gone bad or they'd eaten all of it, thinking it best to save those for an emergency. They had brought kindling upstairs with them that he placed in the sink and set alight, setting a pot on top of it and filling it with the water from the tap, which barely seemed to come out. Once the water had boiled for a full minute, he poured it out into their stores and repeated the process so that they would have enough water for a couple of days. Then, he chopped another tomato and cucumber, already sick of the salad. But he made it anyway, placing some of it on a plate for Nadine and some for himself. She thanked him as she picked at it, looking very introspective.

"Is everything okay?" he asked her.

Looking confused, she looked up at him. "Hmm? Oh, yes. I suppose."

"Is something wrong?" he pressed.

"Well, there are cyborgs trying to kill us, so yes. Of

course."

He cleared his throat briefly. "Yeah. I know. I meant otherwise."

"Yes. I'm fine."

Thinking, he tried to put his concerns into words. "You don't...you don't regret anything, do you?"

Then, she took his hand across the table, smiling slightly. "No. No, I don't," she assured him.

Relieved, he squeezed her hand. "Good. I don't either."

She finished eating her salad, her hand still holding onto his as if she was afraid to let him go. Eventually, she looked up at him and fluttered her lashes, although he wasn't sure if he had just imagined it. "I wouldn't regret doing it again either," she admitted finally.

Although he'd been trying not to think about her, trying not to put any pressure on her to be his companion (not just his roommate), he realized in that moment that he definitely wanted her to be. He pushed his plate aside, leaning across the table to put his arms around her. Then, he just held her, relishing the feeling of her in his arms before he pulled back and kissed her. Part of him wanted to lose himself in the moment, but there was another part of him that feared they would be caught by the cyborgs, and they didn't have long. What if those were his last few minutes on Earth? But if he were to die that evening, he didn't want to spend his last hours full of fear and regret.

Her arms wrapped around him, and he felt incredibly warm and content. He picked her up and carried her to the bed, laying her carefully down on the blankets. His hands reached beneath her blouse, and he stroked her soft skin, gently placing his lips up and down her side before she removed the garment and then slipped off her bra. Her exposed breasts were barely visible in the dim light, but he traced the tip of his tongue along her nipples while she sighed with pleasure. Although it would have been easy to have gotten carried away, he knew it had been a long time since either of them had been intimate with anyone else, and he didn't want to hurt her. The last time, they had been in the darkness. This time, the flashlight provided a small amount of illumination, and he could see her reactions, see that she had a small tattoo of a winged dragon above her right hip. He pressed his lips to it, then waited for her to unbutton his shirt, sliding it off and laying it to one side.

Suddenly, he felt self-conscious, as if she might reject him because she could see his age on him. However, instead of any sort of disapproval, she pulled him toward her, and he could feel her small body beneath his as his mouth sought hers. Her breath came quickly, her heart racing as his hands touched her and made her cry out in ecstasy. "I love you," she whispered. And he wiped away her tears, whispering that he loved her, too.

———

After so long feeling alone, Jackson finally felt he had found someone to care about. He'd cared before, but this was different. Feeling overjoyed in the midst of so much terror, he wished it hadn't taken the apocalypse for him to find her. However, he *had* found her, and he couldn't believe she felt the same for him as he felt for her. For five years, he'd pushed everything down, all of his emotions and all of his desires, until he could almost have convinced himself that he had none. But he did, and he knew, more than anything, that he loved Nadine.

They lay entwined together, her body on top of his, while he ran his fingers through her hair. Of course, at any moment, the cyborgs could appear, but he was glad to have a moment of normality, even if it didn't last. He held onto her as if he knew it wouldn't, as if she might disappear as soon as he released her and then she would be no more. However, he also couldn't imagine being anywhere other than right there at that moment.

He could sense her breathing begin to slow, and then he thought he should probably get a few minutes of sleep before they were racing away across the country again, fleeing the cyborgs that were very obviously hunting them. Closing his eyes, he listened to her breathing for a while, simply content that she was there. But in the back of his mind, the threat was there. He couldn't forget it. Wishing he could find a safe place to hide away with her, he tried to pretend everything was fine, that they were on vacation and getting away from it all. But he knew that wasn't true.

At first, the hum was so soft and soothing that he thought it was Nadine snoring, but then the frequency of it was so familiar and terrifying that he thought he should have realized it from the start. He stood quickly, running to the table to switch off the light, although he was sure it wasn't visible from outside. Then, he climbed into the bed next to Nadine and held her. Her whimper indicated that she had heard it, too, and she was very afraid. "Shh," he tried to whisper comfortingly. "Everything will be fine."

The hum grew louder and louder, and then soon, the

banging sound from the cyborgs' footsteps became more and more apparent. But where was the hum coming from? The last time he'd heard it, they were in Smithton Lake, and the cyborgs had erected a giant dome over the water, which emitted the sound. There wasn't a dome somewhere nearby that he needed to destroy, was there? Neither he nor Nadine had seen such a thing. So where did the sound come from? Was it a clue as to how to destroy the cyborgs?

Nadine shivered in his arms, and he tried to stay calm, tried not to think that they were doomed to die there in that room. The cyborgs seemed to be everywhere, as the sound pervaded the area as if it existed everywhere at once. He thought of his budding relationship, and he didn't want it to end before they could spend their last years together. If the cyborgs were no more, how long would they have? He wasn't sure, but he wanted to find out. He wanted a lifetime more with her, not just a few days.

Were the cyborgs simply looking everywhere, or did they already know where to find him? But if they already knew, how was he still there, sitting terrified in that hotel room? Then, he remembered the way the cyborgs had set fire to the library, and a new fear took hold. What methods were permissible to them? Would they set fire to the hotel, also? Perhaps his anxiety transferred to Nadine because she began trembling more violently than before, and he held her tighter, kissing the side of her face to let her know he was still there and that he cared.

He wanted to apologize for his lapse, but he didn't dare say a word or make a sound. What if he was right, though? What if the cyborgs were pouring out gasoline or whatever they could find and readying a torch right as he sat there thinking about it? Listening for any sign that the cyborgs had stopped, he tried to determine their next move. However, the hum was so intense that he could barely discern anything else. They could be inside the building for all he knew.

The fact that the sound wasn't getting any quieter said the cyborgs were definitely searching, that they suspected Jackson and Nadine were nearby. Jackson waited nervously, listening and watching the blocked window as if he could somehow see beyond the barricades to tell what was happening outside. He didn't hear anything at the front door a few floors below them, but he wasn't sure if he would be able to anyway. They could be blasting it apart with explosives, and he wouldn't be able to hear it.

There was nowhere to go that he and Nadine wouldn't be found, so they sat there terrified and waited for the ordeal to be over. Just because he could hear nothing but the noise of their hunting did not mean the cyborgs couldn't detect him or hear him. His eyes strained in the blackness to see around him, looking for an escape. But he couldn't see anything but the dark. It blanketed the room like a veil. He tried to remember what the room had looked like, what possible hiding places might be present, but it was like a hundred other hotel rooms. They could hide in the bathroom, but that was too obvious. There wasn't enough space under the bed. The armoire was only large enough to hold a small television and nothing else. But they were on the top floor. Was there a crawlspace above? He wasn't sure where the opening would be, however. It was doubtful it would be in his room.

Go away, he thought. Just go away. Hoping that if he

wanted it enough, it would happen, he repeated the words in his mind, repeated them until it seemed they had listened. The sounds grew quieter and quieter as the cyborgs retreated into the distance. A few remained, and he remained still, not moving as the stragglers wandered around the area. He thought he heard something at the door, a sound like the handle was being tried, but whatever it was, it hadn't forced the door open. Then, he thought he heard something else. A voice. A human voice. He couldn't hear the words, but the voice moved away, and then there was only silence.

————

CHAPTER
SIX

"What was that?" Nadine finally dared to ask.

"What?" Jackson asked in return, completely confused.

"Were those people?" she reiterated.

"I don't know. Maybe. But what were they doing? That I couldn't tell you." He leaned his forehead against hers, closing his eyes and feeling grateful that she was still there next to him.

"Do you think they were working with the cyborgs?" she suggested.

He didn't like the idea, but he had wondered that himself. "Maybe."

"What can we do? We can't survive if *everyone* is looking for us." Then, she wept, holding onto him and burying her face into his shoulder.

"We'll figure this out. We did last time." He hoped that was true. There was something strange about the cyborgs this time around, however. They were synchronized and uniform. He didn't know what that meant, but he hoped it suggested a weakness somewhere. Five years earlier, he and Nadine had found the dome that contained the control center for the cyborgs and destroyed the beacon that allowed them to communicate with each other. Were the cyborgs setting up a similar beacon in the trees near the house he shared with Nadine on the beach? Was it the same technology? What if they could find a weakness somehow and destroy it? Would the cyborgs be as vulnerable as before? Or had they developed new defenses?

Tenderly, he extricated himself from Nadine, stopping briefly to brush her tears away with his thumbs before he went to the door, leaning over the table to hopefully see out of the peephole. However, there was nothing visible, and he hoped that whoever had been there before was now gone. The only locked room in the entire hotel was likely to be a giveaway, but he hoped its significance was lost on the intruders.

Coming back to the bed, he took Nadine into his arms again, lying next to her and letting her curl up into his side. "Sleep now. We'll think about all of this in the morning," he urged her. Then, when she was still, and her breathing had slowed, he lay awake, as dreams would not come, and wondered what they could really do to protect themselves.

Jackson analyzed the map, trying to find a route that would keep them away from the larger cities but which might be more secure. Sitting next to him at the small table, Nadine stared over his shoulder at it, periodically making suggestions while he tried to memorize the route and wished he had a highlighter or pencil to mark it. Sometimes he flipped the pages and tried to see if there was anything of note in any of the towns or cities they were going to encounter, but most of it was useless to them without the electrical grid.

Then there was the part of him that was happy with his life on the beach, and he didn't want to get too far from it. Their cottage may not have been a mansion, but it was all he felt he needed. The small space felt safe and comfortable, and he didn't want to give it up just because the cyborgs had returned. In fact, it made him stubbornly cling to the dream as if he had finally found paradise and had it stripped away. It may not have been someone else's idea of perfect, but it was what he wanted. It was *all* he wanted. His life with Nadine was the best thing that could have happened after the end of the world. He couldn't imagine finding anything better anywhere else.

"What do you think about circling back down the coast?" he asked.

"Why?" she replied.

"I don't know. Maybe I don't want to have too far to travel to get home when this is over."

She leaned her head on his shoulder. "Do you really think this will be over someday?"

"There has to be a way to stop them. We did it before."

"This isn't like before," she told him. "They've already wiped most of us out, and we don't have any technology to fight back with."

"I know," he agreed. "I still think we need to take out that beacon they were setting up. If it wasn't important, why set it up at all?"

"Maybe. But we don't know how to do that. What were you thinking?" she asked.

Concentrating on the road atlas, he didn't answer right away. He stared at it, wondering if there was a simple solution he hadn't thought of. Bullets had been ineffective. The cyborgs seemed impervious to fire, so the beacon probably was, too. Then again, he had few resources. What if he could find explosives, though? Would those be enough to blast through whatever force was protecting the beacon? And then, what about the cyborgs left behind? How would he and Nadine destroy them? Her eyes were concerned when he finally looked up from the map as if she thought he hadn't heard her or wasn't going to reply.

"I don't know for sure, but we could try something

basic. I mean, we don't have electricity anywhere anymore. But we could find some explosives and try to blow up the beacon they were setting up near our house," he replied finally.

"Would that be safe?" she worried. "The chemicals might not be stable. It's been five years since almost everything was made."

"That I don't know. I have no experience with them at all. They probably would be very dangerous, but I don't know what else to try."

"What about an acid?" she asked. "We could try something low-tech instead. If we make the acid ourselves, we can be sure it's potent. It might be safer than explosives," she suggested.

"I don't know how to do that, either. Hmm. I guess we can experiment on the cyborg skeleton we brought along. It might give us a clue as to whether it's effective against something they built."

She frowned. "I don't want to bring it in here."

"I wouldn't bring it in here. I think we need to do any experiments outside of our sleeping area anyway. I don't want to have a strong acid or anything nearby just in case there are dangerous fumes." He rubbed his eyes. "I just don't know where to come up with the supplies we might need to create an acid strong enough to do what we want."

She took the map and seemed to stare at it as if it might hold all the answers they needed. "I think we can look around us. Maybe we can just take apart a car battery or something. It has acid in it."

"It's a start," he said. "I still want other options, though.

Don't you think?"

She nodded somewhat reluctantly. "Okay."

"So, we can start with scavenging the area around here and then move on from there. We'll start heading back toward the coast then and make our way back home."

"Okay," she said again, closing the atlas and rising to pick up her overnight bag.

He followed her example, pushing the table back from the door before carefully checking out the peephole for any other intruders. Then, he slipped the atlas into the front pocket of his bag, carrying the bag and his water bottle out the door. Nadine held her weapon ready while Jackson illuminated their way with the flashlight, warily checking to be sure their barricades were undisturbed before they both checked out the back door. Their bikes were still parked there and remained undiscovered, so they went out the door and set their bags in the trailers behind them. Neither of them wanted to check on the cyborg, so they climbed onto their usual bikes, then rode away.

"Do you want to start here or wait until we reach the next town?" Jackson asked as he pulled out of the parking lot.

"The next town," Nadine replied, nervously looking around as if the cyborgs from the night before would suddenly appear.

He had to admit that he was still thinking about the human collaborators, as well, although he didn't want to panic Nadine by talking about it. Then again, perhaps that was the worst thing he could do. Keeping things from her was what had almost destroyed their relationship before it could begin.

They pedaled out of the town and then through the thick trees while Jackson's legs labored to keep his bike up to speed. Even with the wheeled trailer, the cyborg was so heavy that he feared the wheels would break, and he'd simply be dragging the thing along behind him. Bringing it with them seemed to be a bad idea at that moment, and he wished they had a vehicle of some sort that used fuel so that he could still drive around the countryside without using the last of his energy to get around. Even worse, he knew it was on him, as it was his decision to keep it. Although he still recognized it as a stroke of luck, he wondered how he could possibly continue with the trailer barely moving while chained to his bike.

He strained his legs to keep up with Nadine, and now he recognized that it was a safety hazard as well. What if they were pursued? How would he get away? His bike wasn't as maneuverable as before. Even with just his overnight bag, it was difficult, but it wasn't impossible. With the cyborg, it *was* nearly impossible. He could barely keep going, as each turn of the pedals took far more effort than it usually did.

"I'm going to have to do something," he admitted finally, slowing and coming to a halt beside a large boulder and leaning against it.

"What do you mean?" she asked.

"I think I might have to take your advice. We'll have to leave the cyborg somewhere and come back to it. I can't drag it behind me anymore. I'm exhausted."

A slight smirk was the only thing that suggested she had already known that was the case. But concern followed immediately after. "Can you make it to the next town?"

"I'm not sure. I suppose I have to, but I doubt I can go

any farther. It's just too heavy."

She might have offered to take a turn pulling it, but he doubted she would be able to move the weight. She was fairly petite. Instead, he took a few minutes to rest before continuing. He wasn't riding as fast as he had been before, either. All of his effort had been expended in getting to the last town in the time frame they'd had. Now his legs were sore, and he could barely move. They slowly rode down the two-lane road, which led through the pines on either side until a large lake became visible, and then there were signs of old habitation, where houses and hotels had been built at the side of it. It looked like a resort town, with gated entrances along the road on one side and towering hotels and apartments on the other.

"Let's stop here," Jackson pleaded. They saw a large hotel, about eight stories tall, faced in white with elaborate trim around the edges. The name of the hotel had once been on a gilt sign above the entrance, but the gold had faded. The large, curved drive led back from a wall that had once had a water feature in front of it with a reflecting pool and blue colored tiles where water might have trickled over it that was no longer functioning. They rode their bikes into the covered walkway in front of the large brass spinning doors, then Jackson and Nadine did their best to fit their bikes into the space between the doors so that they could bring them inside.

Jackson's flashlight immediately went up, and then Nadine held her weapon ready as they searched. They went downstairs first, checking out the basement and then dumping the contents of Jackson's trailer onto the floor of one of the conference rooms so that he wouldn't have to try to get it upstairs. It only held the cyborg corpse, as he'd since put his overnight bag in Nadine's trailer. Then, they searched the massive kitchens, dining rooms, gym, banquet rooms, and ballrooms on the ground floor. There were so many guest rooms that they were sure it would take all day to search, but they made their way up the stairs, peeking onto each floor before going all the way to the top. They found an elegant presidential suite that was composed of a living room and two bedrooms, each with double doors leading inside. The wallpaper was an eggshell color once, but it had also faded and peeled with time and humidity.

They put their bikes in one of the bedrooms, then rummaged in the small kitchenette for serving utensils and plates. They still had some water from before, so he didn't bother boiling any more yet. Jackson chopped another tomato and cucumber, which were both looking slightly browned in places, but were still edible. Then, he slid one of the plates over to Nadine while they peered out of the giant window at one side of the suite. For security, Jackson wanted to block it off, so they shoved the mattresses from the unused bedroom against the curtains that they pulled closed over it.

Then they shoved the sofa up against the door. Even after turning the deadbolt over, they felt safer that way. The cyborgs could easily break apart the door if they wanted to. But they hoped this hotel had sturdier doors than the others they'd stayed in. Indeed, it appeared far more expensive. Then, Jackson headed for the other bedroom, although there was still some daylight left. The rooms were dark, but he felt far too exhausted to do anything useful. Instead, he curled onto the bed and under the blankets and felt he would fall into a dreamless sleep almost instantly.

Nadine joined him only a couple of minutes later as if she'd taken longer to eat her food than he had. Of course, neither of them had any hobbies, except for Jackson's painting which he could only do at home. Nadine worked in the garden, which she also couldn't do from the hotel. So, they felt slightly bored when they weren't running in fear. Although she didn't seem to be as sleepy as he was, she curled up next to him and put an arm over his prone form on the bed as if wanting to comfort him. Instantly, he felt more cozy and secure. It was as if he could no longer sleep if she wasn't at least in the room, and he felt himself start to doze off as soon as she was near.

———

When Jackson woke, he could barely remember where they were or what had happened. As usual, he felt disoriented and unable to tell the time of day. Shifting slightly, he felt Nadine's weight beside him on the mattress, and he felt reluctant to disturb her. However, his stomach growled, and he knew he probably needed to eat more than just a small amount of salad. But he doubted that Nadine had time to pack any of the salted fish he'd made a few days earlier while still at the beach cottage, which would have provided at least a small amount of protein he probably needed.

He sat up slowly, his head spinning as he was still very, very tired. Finding his way to the bathroom first, he took a brief shower. Part of him missed the warm water and hot showers he used to take, but it did him no good to reminisce as it wasn't something he could get back. Instead, he simply rinsed off and then dried himself before taking care of hygiene. He brushed his teeth with a small amount of the boiled water, shaved, and washed his face. Then, he returned to the bedroom, wanting to lie down again and go back to sleep. However, his hunger was far too irritating, so he went out into the dining area of the suite, finding Nadine already sitting at the table with a plate of food in front of her. As he didn't recognize the plate, he assumed it was from the suite, and he found another in the cabinet before rinsing it thoroughly.

"I don't suppose we have anything but the fruit, do we?" he asked as he sat down.

There was a flashlight sitting bulb up on the table, and she took it and shone it directly on her food, lighting up an array of fruits and preserves, as well as a small amount of the salted fish he'd been sure had been left behind, and some nuts. He smiled. "My savior," he commented as he found her bag and removed the containers with the fish and nuts in them, pouring a small amount of each onto his plate.

"You were distracted," she replied.

"I don't remember," he stated simply.

"You were stocking your trailer with weapons. I went back for some food."

He could barely remember the day they'd left, as if it had been ages earlier. "I'm glad you have more foresight than I do."

"I just wasn't very optimistic. I didn't think we'd be back home that quickly."

That thought made him sad. He wanted to go home, back to the cottage on the beach. It was the closest thing he had any more to a place he belonged, and he was glad to share it with her. "I'm sorry this happened," he told her.

"Why? It wasn't your fault." She was chewing something slowly, thinking. He thought it might have been a bite of the fish.

"Maybe we should try to catch some fish in the lake while we have a chance," he suggested. "It would be nice to have some fresh food."

"We can't cook it, though. We would have to start a fire somewhere," she answered.

He tried to think if there was a place in the hotel where they might be safer instead of cooking the fish in the woods by the water. "Yeah. I'm sure this commercial kitchen is big enough that we can cook it without the risk of fire." The words brought back memories of their escape from the library. He never wanted to see fire ever again.

"Yeah. True," she agreed. She cracked open a peanut shell and crunched on the nuts inside, still focused on her meal, whichever one it was.

"What time is it?" he asked her.

"It's still morning," she replied, and he was glad she always seemed to have an idea.

"Okay, so maybe this afternoon, if nothing happens, we can try to catch a few fish. Maybe there are some edible berries or something in the area, as well. We could, at least, check it out."

She nodded. "That's fine. Maybe some of these houses have some supplies we could use, too."

"Like what?" he asked. He couldn't think of anything they really needed apart from safety and to be rid of the cyborgs forever.

"I don't know. Maybe we could replace our clothes. They're getting holes in them."

He looked down at his shirt, seeing where it was stained and a bit moth-eaten. "Hmm." Perhaps she was right. Staying in hotels did nothing to replenish those types of supplies.

"Maybe one of us can take up weaving and sewing," he suggested, although not seriously.

"You're the creative one," she deadpanned, taking a bite of preserves with her fork.

Puzzled, he tried to determine whether she was upset with him, but then she broke down in giggles, and he realized he had been far too stressed out if he hadn't realized she was joking. He grinned at her, then shook it off. "Maybe one of the houses has a weaving loom and sewing kit. I'll bring it with us for whenever I have time to learn. I might have to learn to spin wool too, come to think of it."

"You will have to wrangle a sheep first. Finding sheep is difficult," she pointed out, perhaps only partly with any solemnity.

He shook his head. "I can use whatever I find, I suppose."

"Dog hair?"

He laughed, finally realizing that she had no intention of forcing him to weave clothes for both of them with nonexistent wool. "Maybe we can use plant fibers?" he suggested, meaning it.

Nodding, she seemed to agree with that assessment. "Perhaps it's worth a try."

"Unless we find some good fabrics in the houses, of course. Then I won't have to worry about learning any new skills for a while."

"Lazy," she giggled, and he laughed again. It felt good to enjoy a moment of conversation without any immediate threat looming. However, he was well aware that the threat could come up without warning, so he still sat relatively quietly, eating his fish jerky and wishing he could have longer with her. But what if they weren't safe where they were hiding in that hotel? He remembered the human collaborators who had almost found them before. If it wasn't just the cyborgs looking for them, he wondered if they would be lucky this time.

———

CHAPTER SEVEN

Walking down the embankment of the lake, apparently called Overton Lake according to the map, they came across a short pier that jutted out over the water and sat down at the end of it. They'd found some fishing rods and equipment at a tackle shop nearby, as they hadn't brought their own rods with them. Then, they cast their lines into the water and waited. Jackson felt edgy. He didn't want to be caught simply trying to meet their basic needs. However, with so few humans in the area, the fish population in the lake must have grown astronomically as they had bites within minutes, the fish desperate for the bait.

When they had a few of them, he put the fish in a bucket he had carried with them, and they hurried back to the relative safety of the hotel, dropping their catch off in the kitchen before setting their rods aside so that they could prepare the food. He had gotten much faster at scaling and gutting the fish through repetition, and he quickly prepared the fillets while Nadine started a small fire in the oven for lack of a better location. Then, they placed the fish on a pan on the oven rack over the flames to cook.

His stomach grumbled, and his mouth watered as he smelled the fish cooking. It was better than cold food, he thought. When it was done, they took the fillets out of the oven and plated them before carrying the dishes upstairs to eat more comfortably before they went out again. They were so hungry by then that they ate all of it within seconds, including their usual tomato and cucumber salad as a side. Jackson thought it was the best fish he'd ever eaten, although he could barely remember a time before the arrival of the cyborgs when he'd had fish before, anyway.

They washed up and changed, then headed down to the hotel gift shop. There, they gathered a few plastic bags to use to carry anything they managed to scavenge, then they went downstairs and crossed the street to the driveway of the first of the gated lake houses. It wasn't a large house, but it was appointed luxuriously, and Jackson almost wished they'd decided to hide there. But he knew it would be more difficult to secure thoroughly in so short a time, so they decided to remain at the hotel. They walked through the house, which sported a wall of glass on one side and was tiled in white marble on the other. Although it allowed a magnificent view of the lake, it was vulnerable to attack by the cyborgs, and there was minimal furniture in that room with which to barricade the wall-size window.

When they went into the bedroom, they found a large walk-in closet full of once-expensive clothes, which they hoped would be in better condition than the items they had with them. Of course, cotton fabrics had degraded heavily over time, so they especially looked at anything with synthetic materials, which had fared better. Nadine found a few blouses and dresses, which weren't in her size, but that would do, and she stuffed them into her bags. Jackson wanted clothes that were comfortable to work in, but the homeowner mostly possessed dress shirts and suits. It wasn't ideal, but Jackson knew he needed something better than what he had. He put a few of the polo shirts into his bags and hoped the pants would fit well enough, as he also took a couple of belts as insurance.

After thoroughly searching the house, they ran back to the hotel with their finds, hoping to rid themselves of the clothes they no longer needed. Nadine immediately stripped out of the stained and ripped blouse she'd been wearing and headed to take a shower as if she couldn't stand the thought of putting clean clothes on herself after she'd been sweating so much. Jackson felt the same. The shirt he had on was pretty ragged, and he debated changing anyway or waiting until Nadine returned.

Then, he heard her sing. Maybe she had done it since he'd met her, but he'd never heard it before as she never did so in his presence. She sang a few lines of "Moonlight Becomes You," her voice clear and ringing over the sound of the water. Suddenly, he felt entranced, and he slowly made his way to the door, opening it slightly so that he could hear her, unable to see her behind the curtain. She'd left a flashlight on the counter so that she wasn't in complete darkness, and he stepped forward, casting a shadow along the curtain, and she immediately froze.

"Is that you, Jackson?" she called out.

"Yeah," he replied shyly. "I've never heard you sing before."

The curtain pulled aside slightly, and she peeked out with a slight grin. "You want to join me?"

In that instant, he felt he couldn't have resisted if he'd wanted to. He stripped out of the old garments and slipped into the shower beside her. Her arms wrapped around him as he stepped under the water, and then her fingers were working the shampoo that she had made the week before into his hair. It felt extravagant and intoxicating, the scents of lavender and vanilla mingling in the air around him. When she resumed the song, all he could think of was that he wanted her, that he couldn't believe she was his. He could have kissed her, but then the song would be over, so he stood there and allowed her to lather soap over his body and fuss over him like a child.

Afterward, he felt impossibly clean, and although he watched her longingly as she dried herself with a towel, he didn't want to spoil the experience. It was far more intimate than he had expected. Then, they returned to the bedroom and lay on the bed under the blankets, Nadine's hair wet and leaving damp spots on the pillows. All he wanted to do was touch her, and he ran his fingers over her skin tenderly and affectionately, trying to convey without words how he felt about her. She leaned into him and closed her eyes while he stroked her side and ran his fingers through her hair. She really was unbelievably beautiful, he thought, overwhelmed with emotion.

Then a thought occurred to him. "What day is today?" he asked her.

"I don't know," she mumbled.

"The date," he pressed.

"I think it's November fifteenth."

He slid from the covers, hearing her grumble disappointedly as he dug around in his overnight bag. When he returned, he lay next to her again, but his hand sought hers, and he placed a small round object in her fingers and gazed at her intently. "I didn't forget," he told her.

"Forget what?" she wanted to know.

"Your birthday. I know it's not important anymore to have anything like that, and the craftmanship isn't the best. But I wanted to make something for you. Something as beautiful as you are. I failed in that aspect, but I hope you like it."

Opening her hand, she could see a white outline, a flat disk resting in the middle of her palm. She traced her finger over it and felt the engraving. Then, she rose and took the object into the bathroom to see it by the light. When she re-entered the room, she still had the flashlight with her, and she smiled as she stared at the disk. It had a small hole at the top where a leather cord ran through it, so she let it dangle from her fingers, watching it glow as the light caught the pendant he had carved by hand from a seashell. As there were no seashells anywhere that they'd been, she knew he must have made it days or maybe even weeks before.

She lay beside him again, reaching behind her so that he could fasten the cord around her neck. "Thank you," she said finally as if the words wouldn't come to her before. "It's beautiful."

He could see the pendant as it gleamed against her skin, and he could see all the flaws, all the mistakes he'd made. Her words meant everything to him. Her approval was all that mattered. But he felt she deserved something better as if he could have made her a pair of diamond earrings or some such thing. Taking them from a house was too simple, however. It took no effort to obtain something like that, and so it wouldn't adequately show how much he cared. Although he'd practiced with other materials before he'd carved the seashell, he knew he hadn't made a perfect work of art.

"Really?" he asked, still doubtful that she was being honest with him, that she really liked it.

"Yeah. No one has ever made anything for me before." She turned to face him, the light behind her now, and she kissed him deeply before pulling back and attempting to admire the pendant again.

He felt relieved that the gesture was appreciated and that she understood the meaning of the gift. "I'm glad you like it."

There was a floral pattern carved over the surface of the shell, as he knew how much she loved the garden, and he watched her run her fingers over it as she stared, hopefully not picking it apart to find his errors. "I didn't know you could do this."

"I taught myself. I broke a few before I made that one," he admitted.

She giggled in response. "I love it."

But he wasn't sure if she meant she loved his story or the relatively intact shell he'd given her.

———

Needing protective gloves before they took apart a car battery, they searched the nearby area on their bikes for an auto repair shop or something of that sort. When they found it, they only hoped there would be supplies left behind. However, they could find nothing of the sort, as if people who lived near Overton Lake never had car problems. Jackson was about to give up on the endeavor when he saw a glass-blowing studio. He pointed in that direction, and Nadine followed him toward the studio, which boasted an attached gallery. A few of the vessels had survived, although they were covered in a thick layer of dust. Although they wanted to glimpse a few of them, they didn't want to touch the dust with their bare fingers. So, they walked back toward the studio through a back door behind the reception desk.

Inside, Jackson tilted the flashlight toward the large

furnace, which was no longer operational, but which had a scattering of items in front of it, as if the artists had left in a rush (or worse). On one wall was mounted a series of storage lockers, like in a school, but most of the doors were still hanging open. He hurried over to search them, finding a pair of leather gloves and some tools for handling the hot, melted glass. It seemed only logical that they might be useful to handle acid, as well. If he were wrong, he hoped the rest of the gear would protect him.

There were goggles, heavy aprons, and other protective equipment that he stowed in a plastic bin he found, then carried all of it out to the waiting bikes, where he put the bin into his trailer. Nadine had wrapped something in a layer of felt, and he could only assume it was one of the glass sculptures. Although he felt curious, he knew the fragile object would likely shatter long before they could ever get it home.

Approaching the hotel, they managed to get their bikes into the foyer, then they removed the bin from Jackson's trailer and carried it up all of the flights of stairs until they reached the top floor where their suite was located. By that time, it was getting late, and dusk was falling, so they were leery of being out in the dark and carrying bright lights that would only draw attention to them. Tomorrow, Jackson told himself. They flopped onto the sofa after shoving it in front of the door, feeling tired, but hoping they would make some sort of progress soon. Although the area was obviously a resort town, they were not on vacation.

"What did you find in there?" Jackson asked, holding Nadine in his arms while they rested.

"I just wanted to see what one of those sculptures

looked like," she replied sheepishly as if he might scold her.

"Okay. Let's look at it," he answered instead.

She grinned, then fetched the bundle, which she'd set on the floor to one side of the door. He took it to the bathroom, where he unwrapped it carefully, trying to avoid scattering the dust into the air. Then, he turned the water on in the sink, where he set the small vessel, about six inches tall and about four inches wide, flared at the top. He rinsed the dust off carefully, wiping away the black and gray substance and then gently foaming soap over the surface. Nadine held the flashlight over it as he worked, and the vessel seemed to glow from within as the dust was washed away, the sink bathed in red and gold where the light passed through, causing patterns of light and shadow to play on the wall behind him.

Seeing the now-clean vase, he set it on the counter and dried it with a towel, watching the beam of light reflect on it as Nadine admired it. "It's amazing!" she cried.

Now that he could see it properly, it was a dark eggplant at the base, but it gradually lightened to scarlet and then gold at the top. Although it was mostly conical, it had a fluted edge reminiscent of a morning glory. "It is," he agreed, then he wrapped it in a blanket, hoping to save it so that she could find a place for it in their house. Even though it wasn't likely the vase would make the journey intact, he would do whatever he could to protect it for her as she seemed to have fallen in love with it.

She placed the bundle in her overnight bag, where it was further cocooned in her clothing and other possessions. Then, she lay on the bed, taking the flashlight with her and turning it off to conserve the batteries. Jackson joined her, feeling bored now that the minor excitement was over. Sighing deeply, he turned over onto his back and lay there, staring into the darkness and wishing things were settled so that they wouldn't have to worry about the cyborgs any longer. Nadine turned to face him and draped her arm over his chest, then she lazily toyed with the buttons on the front as if she were distracted.

Before, he would have found the gesture comforting, a sign that things were returning to normal, but he knew that wasn't the case. Instead, it filled him with a longing for the life that had been stolen from him when the cyborgs returned. Things had been comfortable, if not idyllic, or at least as much as they could have been under the circumstances. As much as he felt grateful for Nadine and the new phase in their relationship, he would never thank the cyborgs for taking away their chance for peace. He would have waited years if that's what it took, for her to feel at ease with him because he didn't want to force the issue. Although she'd initiated the whole endeavor, he still felt a sense of guilt because it had not happened through natural means, or at least not what he deemed as such.

And then, although he was fatigued beyond words, he found he couldn't relax. Instead, he *listened*. Because the cyborgs would likely find them eventually, he knew they wouldn't stop looking as long as there were survivors. Then, he thought of his and Nadine's bikes, brought inside the hotel where they weren't visible from the road. At least the lobby had been more spacious at this hotel, and the bikes would fit this time. However, he worried their hiding place wouldn't be too hard to find, and he hoped they had more time to work on a defense (or offense if they could figure out a weakness).

A low wail, almost like a siren, gradually grew in volume outside the building, and he feared they'd been found. Quietly, he disentangled himself from Nadine's embrace and tiptoed across the room until he reached the window, worried they would need to somehow escape the hotel unseen. However, as loud as the sound was, he could only see movement in the distance, far away from the town. Several sorts of flying craft, smooth, oblong and sleek silver shapes, were hovering above the mountainside, what looked like searchlights slowly moving over the ground below them. The craft shifted, and the wind picked up as if they relied on the air to keep aloft, and then they all seemed to converge on a point. They'd found what they were looking for. A bright green beam shot downward from one of the flying machines, and then the ground below it exploded downward, a crater appearing where there had once been trees.

Jackson held onto Nadine, who was horrified and tried to keep her silent. They watched, mesmerized, as the craft continued to hover over the site as if confirming their target had been destroyed. Then, they shot away, moving faster than a human aircraft could have. Jackson didn't dare move, afraid any change would somehow attract the spacecraft to their position. He tried desperately to slow his breathing, to convince himself that nothing had happened. But he knew without checking that someone had died. Why else would the cyborgs have been there and blasted anything at all? That was their only goal. The cyborgs had found survivors and terminated them. Would he and Nadine be next?

———

CHAPTER EIGHT

Outside the hotel, Jackson and Nadine roamed the parking lot with a glass container from the kitchen that would hopefully help them contain any chemicals they were able to find. Both of them wore the protective equipment they'd gathered from the glass studio, hoping to minimize any danger, although they weren't sure yet how to turn the acid into a weapon, should it be effective. They only knew they had to start somewhere, and projectile weapons were completely harmless to the cyborgs and their technology.

Finding a large black SUV parked near the door, Jackson smashed the window so that he could toggle the release for the hood. Then, he lifted the panel and carefully scrubbed the corrosion from the battery's terminals with a wire brush so that he could better see what he needed to do. Once that was done, he loosened the cables and slid them off the terminals to remove the battery from the vehicle. As it was completely sealed, he made sure his gloves were on securely and that his face shield was down before he took the various tools and attempted to take apart the outer casing.

In the end, the task required both of them to complete, with Jackson holding the battery still while Nadine pried the casing apart. A small amount of acid spilled onto his leather apron, but he was miraculously uninjured. He upturned the battery over the glass container he'd set on the ground beside the SUV. It was a disappointingly small amount after all the effort it had taken to obtain it, and he began to worry that their plan wasn't very feasible as a way to defend themselves. It would take hours or possibly days to collect enough acid to use against a large number of cyborgs, and they didn't have enough storage for more than a small amount.

Sighing, he draped a rubber mat over the glass container to keep it from spilling as he carried it back toward the hotel and then down the stairs into the basement where they'd left the inactive cyborg corpse they'd recovered. Still wearing the protective gear, he lifted the container and removed the cover, carefully standing back before he poured a small amount onto the center of the skeletal frame. The acid bubbled and sizzled as it struck the metal. However, several seconds later, it had only etched a shallow pattern of lines where it had run down the sides and left black marks on the carpet below. Frustrated, he grumbled as he watched the acid slowly eat away at the outer surface, barely doing any damage at all.

"Well, that was pointless," he complained.

"We didn't know what it would do. Now we know," she snapped back.

Realizing that his comment might have sounded like a criticism of her plan, he had to admit she was right. "Yeah. We needed to experiment. We've done that. What else can we try?" He wanted to sit down, but the floor of the basement didn't look very comfortable, and especially not with all the gear he was wearing.

She kicked at the cyborg lightly with her foot as if she still weren't sure it wouldn't come alive at some point, even after they'd tried to destroy it with acid, and it had not yet moved. "We should go back upstairs," she suggested warily.

"Yeah," he agreed, heading toward the stairs. As soon as he could see her flashlight move toward him, he began to ascend the levels up to the top floor. He knew she was behind him as the beam of her light illuminated the steps in front of him. When he reached the fifth floor, his breathing was a little ragged, but he managed to open the door before stripping out of the apron, face shield, and other gear. Nadine's equipment crashed to the floor behind him before she collapsed onto the sofa.

"We should push that in front of the door," he reminded her, and she stood to help him move the furniture again. Once it was back in place, she lay heavily against the cushions while he took her water bottle from the table and handed it to her. She took it gratefully and sipped from it while he searched for his own. When he found it, he returned to the living room and sat beside her.

With her lying her head on his shoulder, he tried to think of an alternative to fighting the cyborgs, who had previously made it clear they would not share the planet with humans, so he didn't think they would compromise when they were clearly winning the battle. But he didn't have any clue how to fight them if it came to that. All he knew was that there was a beacon somewhere, but he wasn't sure of its purpose or how to disable it. However, it was important, or the cyborgs wouldn't have set it up at all.

Nadine didn't say a word, only sipped her water as she leaned against him. Perhaps she knew he was thinking, trying to solve their shared dilemma. Or perhaps she was trying to solve it, too. Neither wanted to die, and certainly not at the hands of the alien beings that simply tore people apart like they were made of paper. Jackson knew Nadine still thought of David, even if she rarely mentioned him anymore. It wasn't that she'd forgotten. Surely, she thought of David every day. However, she didn't want the day of his murder to be the only way she remembered him. Jackson was aware that everyone he cared about from his previous life was most likely dead, probably murdered the same way David was. But he hadn't witnessed the event the way Nadine had. It wasn't his last memory of each of them. It would be harder for her to think of David without seeing the image of his dismemberment in her mind.

Taking her hand, he stroked the back of it with his thumb and hoped this wasn't the end, that they didn't only have a few moments left, and that was all. He knew he wasn't a replacement for David, but he hoped that he could somehow fill the void left behind when David had died, or at least that he could make David's absence less painful. Five years was a long time, but it also wasn't. It had flown by, a blur that barely made an impression on his mind except for the hardships he'd faced with Nadine. But it wasn't all bad. Now all he could think about was Nadine and keeping her happy and safe. However, who was he to think he was the right person for that? Could he really protect her the way he wanted to? Only time would tell.

They walked through the parking lot, heading toward the site where they'd seen the cyborgs the night before. Hoping they were less likely to be spotted on foot, they headed across the mountainside and down into the valley. Jackson tripped over tree roots and slipped on piles of leaves, fearing every sound echoed through the trees like a klaxon. Nadine seemed more at ease, nearly silent, as she placed her feet carefully with each step. He tried to follow her lead, but his feet felt clumsy as he stumbled and tromped over the ground. A couple of times, he caught her glare at him over her shoulder as he accidentally cursed, stubbing his toe. Point taken, he thought.

Once they reached the bottom of the valley, they knew they had to climb up the other side. The cyborgs had been on the opposite side of the mountain in front of them as they hadn't been able to see everything that was happening from their hotel room. The side was steep, so Jackson helped Nadine up into the trees, where she then pulled him up behind her. Then, they both slowly climbed, sometimes on all fours to keep from falling down, up and up, until they neared the top of the ridge. They didn't need to go all the way to the mountain's peak but around the side, so they only headed about halfway up before climbing around through the trees and other obstacles until they'd rounded the edge of it and could no longer see where they'd come from.

When they had cleared the ridge, it was obvious where the cyborgs had been. There was a wide swath of trees missing, *obviously* missing, from the forest below them. In their place was a shallow pit full of black ash that covered several hundred square feet. However, in their caution, they did not notice any cyborgs or any of their technology left behind. There was only the pit and silence. Jackson crept forward, kneeling beside the depression in the ground, while Nadine stayed motionless behind him. His hand reached out, but he could feel heat still rising off the ash, and he pulled it back.

A sound to his right startled him, and he jumped up to run away. But then, he could hear a light sobbing, and he knew it wasn't a threat. Looking over, he saw a woman holding onto two small children, only toddlers. She had a tear-streaked face covered in mud or ash, and her children were swaddled in blankets beside her. One of them seemed to be wearing only pajamas, but he appeared to be only about two years old, so he was born after the cyborgs had left the first time. The other was a young girl, about four years old, who wore a tutu and a plastic tiara as if she'd been playing dress-up before the cyborgs had returned and she hadn't yet decided to take off the accessories.

The woman, possibly no more than twenty-five years old, looked terrified as she caught sight of Jackson, and she froze, not daring to move in case he hadn't actually seen her. Or maybe she was waiting to see what he would do. Maybe she was too frightened to run. He looked back at Nadine, whose face was suddenly full of compassion and empathy.

"It's okay," Jackson said to the woman. "We're not going to hurt you."

She stood there and didn't say a word, only holding onto her children and shivering.

"Were you here last night?" Nadine asked.

The woman nodded, and her lips pressed together before more tears streamed down her cheeks. She looked about to speak, but no words would come out.

"You knew someone," Jackson stated plainly. She nodded again. "I'm sorry." He looked back the way he'd come with Nadine. "Where are you staying? You can't sleep out here. They'll find you."

"I don't want to leave my...husband," the woman cried.

"Is he coming back for you?" Jackson asked.

"I don't know."

"Where did he go?" Nadine inquired gently.

"He was right there," the woman replied, pointing to the center of the pit. "He was right there."

Nadine took a few steps forward and approached the woman, who recoiled slightly but then resigned herself to her fate. "I'm Nadine. What's your name?"

"Mayra," the woman answered.

"Nice to meet you. I'm Jackson," Jackson introduced himself. "Why don't you come with us? We're staying on the other side of that mountain. You don't want to be here when they come back."

"No. But what about Ramón? I don't want to leave him," Mayra argued.

Jackson didn't know how to tell her kindly that Ramón was likely dead. "Why don't you wait with us? We can come back to look for him tomorrow."

"No. What if he comes back tonight?" Mayra fretted.

"He was in the center of the beam of light?" Nadine asked.

"Yes. But he wouldn't leave me," Mayra insisted.

"Maybe not intentionally. The cyborgs most likely took him. I'm sorry," Nadine told Mayra, probably hoping a small, white lie was easier to accept than the truth.

"No!" Mayra protested. "What will I do?"

"Come with us for now," Jackson suggested. "At least you can make sure your children are safe while you think about it."

Mayra looked down at the small forms huddled under the blankets and nodded, agreeing. She stood to her full height, hefting a large tote bag onto her shoulder, and urged the toddlers forward. They climbed back up the mountain, reversing their path and heading back toward the hotel. The children seemed to think of it as almost a game, racing each other up the steep incline while the adults struggled to keep up. But, by the time they reached the bottom of the valley, Jackson had picked up the four-year-old while Mayra held the young boy. Continuing on their journey, they fought their way up the mountain, seeing the back of the hotel up ahead. Then, they doubled their efforts, knowing rest was a few minutes away.

As soon as they reached the parking lot, however, Jackson held everyone back. He didn't want to be complacent, especially when they were so tired. So, he walked around the building at a distance, then signaled everyone else forward when he was sure the coast was clear. Everyone hurried inside the building, and Jackson helped Mayra settle into one of the rooms on the lower level (at her request) before he left to rest in the suite he shared with Nadine. He wasn't sure Mayra would stay where he'd left her, but he hoped she wouldn't risk everyone's safety by leaving to look for her husband.

"Where is she?" Nadine asked Jackson when he'd returned.

"She's in 102. She didn't want to be on a higher floor because she still thinks her husband is out there somewhere."

That thought soured Nadine's expression, and she looked sad. "Do you think he's gone?"

"I doubt he survived that. It flattened and burned the trees and left a crater behind. If he was standing where she said he was standing, he's got to be dead."

She frowned more than before. "So, how can we stop them if they have those weapons? They don't even have to come near us to kill us."

"I don't know."

———————

Jackson thought he heard a rumbling sound in the distance, but when he woke, he realized it was just Nadine snoring beside him, her lips almost touching his ear. Relieved, he sat up, then went to the bathroom with one of the flashlights. He splashed water on his face from the sink, feeling tense. However, the action brought him back to reality, and he returned to the bed, carefully feeling around with his hands to make sure he didn't hurt Nadine when he lay down again. Unfortunately, he still managed to clock her on the side of her head as he swung his hand across in the darkness, and he heard her quiet, "Oof," as he winced and found an open space on the mattress.

"Sorry," he told her, hearing her groan as she woke up.

"For what?" she mumbled.

"For waking you by punching you. It was clearly unintentional."

She managed a giggle in response, even as he heard her yawn. "A likely story," she teased him, meaning the opposite.

"There are other ways I'd rather wake you," he insisted. And then she laughed out loud, barely able to control the impulse.

"Like what? Name one," she said through her laughter.

"Tell you or show you?" he asked mischievously. Then, the most unwelcome knock in the universe sounded on their door. It had to be Mayra.

Jackson growled as he sat up, feeling disappointed, although he was sure Nadine shared his sentiment. He slipped a shirt on and stumbled into a pair of pants as the knock sounded again. He thought he heard a muffled, "Are you there?" from outside the door as he tried to reach it without bumping into the furniture.

"Yes, yes. I'm coming," he called out, although he didn't want to shout. Not sure she heard him, he unlocked and then opened the door, although, with the barricade, it only opened about an inch. "Can I help you?"

Mayra stood in the hallway with her two young children hiding behind her skirt. "Do you have any food?" she asked, then she suddenly shook her head. "Not for me. For my children. They're hungry."

Then, Jackson could see how thin Mayra had gotten. It was obvious now that he saw it. Her clothes barely hung onto her slender frame, and she had dark circles under her eyes, the signs that she'd been giving her food to her children and starving herself for their survival. However, he also knew that he and Nadine barely had enough food for themselves. But he couldn't find it in himself to say no, to reject Mayra and her children when he had plenty to eat over the previous several days, and they had not.

"I'll bring you a plate. But there are fishing rods in the shop downstairs. You should probably take one while you can. That's what we did."

"I can't catch anything," Mayra countered. "My husband did that."

"We don't have enough to feed you," Jackson told her sadly. "I can give you something right now, but if Ramón doesn't return, you will have to feed these children somehow."

"He wouldn't leave us," she argued, still standing in

the hall.

"No. He might not have wanted to, but the cyborgs probably took him. You might have to accept that he's gone and—"

"No. I won't. Never mind. I'll find something to eat elsewhere." Her chin went up before she spun around to leave, a sign that he'd insulted her pride somehow.

"Look. I'll give you a plate. Just wait there. I'll teach you to fish in the lake this afternoon."

Shyly, she turned back, an expression of hope beginning to show on her face. "Really?"

"Yes. Nadine and I can show you. It's not that difficult. I'm sure you can do it."

Mayra looked down at her charges, seeming to come to a decision. "Okay. I'll wait for you."

He closed the door while he foraged in their food stores to make a plate large enough for the three of them, but that wouldn't put himself and Nadine at a disadvantage. Of course, it wouldn't hurt Nadine and him to go out to the lake to fish if their stores were getting that low anyway. Perhaps it was a good thing. He put servings of nuts and berries in with the salted fish and some of the preserves, then he pushed the sofa out of the way so that he could hand the plate out to Mayra. She thanked him profusely, and the children's eyes lit up on seeing the food.

"Later this afternoon, we'll go to the lake. Wait for us," he reiterated.

Mayra nodded, then turned to leave, the children's voices clamoring for attention as she headed for the stairwell. Jackson closed the door, locked it, and pushed the sofa against it again. When he finally returned to the bedroom, Nadine was in the shower, however, and all hope of any romance was gone. Then again, he knew he probably had more important things to do. Quickly, he gathered up their belongings and began to clean the plates they'd used. Then, he started to rinse their dirty clothes with soap, leaving them to soak for a few minutes while he tidied the rest of the rooms, making sure they could leave in a hurry if they needed to. But why were they still undiscovered at the hotel? Would their luck hold out?

———

CHAPTER NINE

Mayra listened while Jackson took her around the nearby shop, gathering equipment and showing her what she needed to have to catch fish. She seemed earnest like she was really paying attention, but she had half an eye on her children, watching out for them. Jackson felt like it was a lost cause. She still thought Ramón would return and take care of everything the way he'd always done.

Jackson picked out a tackle box and began packing different lures, floats, and weights, insisting this was important as he placed everything in a different compartment for easy organization. Then, he tried to explain what everything was for, when she would need it and when she wouldn't, but she didn't seem to be interested any longer. She called to the children as they raced around the store and tried to keep them from knocking over store displays, although there was no one around to be annoyed by their behavior except Jackson and Nadine.

Finally, he gave up and took his own equipment out of the store and headed to the lake. Nadine trailed behind, her own gear carefully stowed as she walked out the door. She didn't look back, but Mayra and the children seemed to take this as their cue to begin crying. "You had better come along, or you'll miss everything," Nadine chided Mayra.

Jackson was halfway to the lake when they joined him. This time, Mayra had the tackle box he'd begun packing, and she had picked out a fishing rod and reel, although he wasn't sure she'd listened to the lecture at all. But she had stopped crying, and she had a determined look on her face that gave him a little bit more confidence than he'd had before.

Eventually, they approached the water's edge, peering

through the trees first to be sure they had not been observed. Jackson showed Mayra what to do to get started, how to bait her hook and how to cast it into the water. Her movements were clumsy, but she managed to get her line in the lake a few feet from his. He wished it were a little farther away, but perhaps there were plenty of fish in the lake after all. There were few predators anymore. Only the ones hunting humans.

It wasn't long before Jackson and Nadine had caught several fish, but with Jackson helping, Mayra had caught a couple of them, too. They carried their catch back toward the hotel, freezing when they saw a large crowd of people gathered outside the front door. Mayra called out, to Jackson's chagrin, and then she ran toward them with open arms. "Do you need a place to stay? There's room inside."

Jackson looked over his shoulder, and Nadine's expression surely echoed his own. He hurried to the door, where Mayra was ushering the strangers into the lobby. Catching up to her, he took her shoulder and nearly shouted at her, "What are you doing?"

"I thought there was plenty of room," she argued.

"Only if the cyborgs don't find us. Do you think we'll be undiscovered long with all these people coming and going?" he countered.

"I can't just leave them out here," she said stubbornly.

"Do you know these people?" he asked incredulously. "You *invited* them here?"

Sheepishly, she dropped her gaze to her feet. "Yes."

He couldn't control his eye-roll, and he bit his lip to keep from screaming at her. "This was private, and we were undiscovered up until now. We only asked you to come inside because of your children, but you can't invite an entire town to come stay here. We'll be discovered."

"It isn't an entire town," she snapped. "They're my relatives."

"I don't care who they are. No more. We might not be safe here anymore," he told her angrily. "You'll need to barricade the doors and windows on this floor now. Keep everyone quiet, and no one else comes or goes. Make sure the cyborgs won't be able to tell anyone is here."

She glared at him, but she nodded. Jackson led Nadine toward the stairwell, fuming, and then he climbed up to the fifth floor with his anger keeping him from getting overly winded. He grumbled the entire way, and Nadine didn't say anything to him. Once they were back in their suite, they locked the door and shoved the sofa against it, Jackson almost dumping the fish into the sink with the laundry in his haste. Then, he quickly drained the sink, cleaned it out, and moved the laundry to the bathtub instead. By the time he returned, she had already begun gutting the fish they'd caught.

"The nerve of that woman," he complained, pacing, as there wasn't space for him to help in the small kitchen. "Do you believe her?"

"She only wanted to help her family. Do you blame her?" Nadine said indulgently.

He sighed. "I know. But you understand my point too, don't you?"

"Of course, I do," she agreed.

"So, am I wrong? I just want to keep us safe. I don't think we can do that if there is a large group staying here."

"No. You're right. I just understand why she did what

she did."

He sat down on the sofa, twisting around so that he could see her from his vantage point. "Do you think I overreacted?"

She shook her head, even as she worked to finish with the fish as quickly as she could. "No. She needs to realize the world doesn't revolve around her."

"You would think that the last five years might have taught her that." Grunting, he lay back against the cushions, frustrated that the situation was now out of his control and not for the better.

Nadine packed the fish in a glass crock between layers of salt from the kitchen, then she took the bag she'd dumped the detritus into and took it into the hallway to dispose of it, waiting briefly for Jackson to unbarricade the door so that she could get out. When she returned, he looked up from his spot on the sofa as if he'd been afraid something bad might have happened to her.

"I need another shower," she complained as she headed toward the bathroom.

He stopped to block the door again before following her into the bedroom. She'd stripped out of her dirty clothes and stood there staring at him, naked and smelling like fish. "Me, too," he added, and he copied her actions before she opened the bathroom door to start the shower.

"Laundry!" he called out, remembering. It was too late. The clothes that he'd wrung out were now soaking wet again, sitting in the bottom of the tub where she had, by then, shut off the water, but the damage was done. She pulled each item out and dumped it into the sink before turning the water on again.

"Come in," she told him, and he carefully stepped into the shower, missing hot water terribly. But by now, he was used to the cold. There was nothing to do about it where they were. He couldn't heat water with the fire pit to put into the bath as he had done in their cottage.

Seeing her body dripping with soap and water, he wanted to wrap his arms around her, but she had him sit down while she shampooed his hair, trying to get the foul fish odor out of it. She then scrubbed her skin furiously, leaving red marks where she'd used too much pressure. He offered to help with a gesture, and then she sat next to him while he lathered her skin and hair and helped her to rinse without getting any of it in her eyes. When he kissed her, she shut off the water again, and then she entwined her arms around him, her skin cold and damp, where drops of water ran off her hair and onto her shoulders. He could taste the soap she'd used, the floral scent tickling his nose and causing him to want her more.

Then, he was lost. Lost because he couldn't ever see a way out of the love that he'd built around her. But he didn't want to. He'd waited five years to tell her. Five years of contentment, and he wanted more. All he knew was that she was there with him, and he hoped he would never be without her for as many days as he still had left on Earth.

———

That night, he heard them. The ground trembled and shook as the cyborgs approached the hotel and surrounded it. He would have cursed, but he feared making a sound. Even five floors up, he wasn't sure how well the cyborgs could hear or detect movement. Obviously, the crowd outside the hotel the day before had attracted the cyborgs' attention, and Jackson worried they wouldn't leave when morning came.

This time, they didn't march or walk around. They knew exactly where they were going. The cyborgs stood at attention, all facing the building and then watching. Waiting. Jackson crept from the bed at the relative silence, hoping they'd actually gone. But when he peered out around the barricade against the window, he could see thousands of glowing red eyes staring back at him. Chilled, he felt his heart skip a beat at the sight. Did they know people were hiding inside the hotel? It was obvious they knew something was there that interested them. But what did they intend to do? Would they just wait until someone left to look for food? Or would they storm the building? Jackson remembered the fire at the library, and he worried that he and Nadine would be forced out, one way or another.

She'd tiptoed up behind him, and he felt her hand on his shoulder before he could turn to face her. He brought his lips close to her ear and whispered, "They're outside." He didn't need to see her expression to know she was terrified.

He felt her shiver, and then her breaths were shaky as she whispered in reply. "Can we get out?"

Shaking his head, he knew the movement would be sensed in the air, even if she couldn't see him. He put an arm around her before she could break down before she could collapse onto the floor in tears. Then, he led her to the sofa to sit down, where they huddled together in the darkness and waited to see what would happen. The silence was almost more unbearable than the noise when the cyborgs were still searching for survivors. Jackson knew they were caught and couldn't get away this time. But this wasn't how he wanted his story to end.

How could they get out without being spotted? Would the cyborgs eventually give up and walk away? That was doubtful. They didn't have the emotions required to tire of any sort of assault. They didn't have the physical weaknesses that humans had in their metallic bodies, either. They could keep it up indefinitely. The survivors in the hotel were at a definite disadvantage. They would require food eventually. They would need to leave. Or the cyborgs would force them out. Did they stand any chance at all? Jackson didn't want to give up, but he feared this was the end.

His terror kept him from going back to sleep. Nadine shuddered beside him, silently weeping even as he tried to comfort her. But what could he say? Could he guarantee they would survive, that they would be okay? That was the only thing that mattered, really. Anything else he told her would be pointless and trite. And she didn't want him to lie, surely.

Eventually, he felt drawn back to the window, and he stood shakily on his feet as he walked across the room again. She followed him, understandably scared of being separated. When he peeked out the window, however, the scene looked much the same, if not exactly. The cyborgs hadn't moved, that he could tell, and they still stood staring at the hotel. Then, suddenly a figure ran out the front door, which was hopefully barricaded again behind him. The man tried to flee, and one cyborg stepped out of formation to grab him. Suddenly, Jackson put his hand out to cover Nadine's eyes. He knew what was coming. The cyborg ripped the man's head from his body in one quick motion, the rest of the man's body collapsing onto the ground before another cyborg picked it up, and then the two of them tore off the limbs, blood spurting copiously onto the ground. In the darkness outside, the blood appeared almost black as it spilled out onto the concrete. Then, the cyborgs stepped back and returned to their previous positions, standing still and staring. Just staring.

Jackson wanted to get the image out of his mind, wanted to turn back time and turn away before he could see what the man's fate had been. But he couldn't forget the man's screams as he had tried to escape and the way the sound had cut off so abruptly. Jackson had watched, horrified, as the cyborgs had destroyed the corpse as if humans could come back to life if their bodies were left intact. Perhaps the cyborgs could. It was a clue, but one that pointed to their infallibility rather than a weakness.

And then, he remembered. What about the inactive cyborg he'd left in the basement? A bad feeling came over him, although he wasn't sure what it was exactly. He hurried back to the door, grabbing a flashlight on his way. Then he pushed the sofa aside, and he and Nadine ran down the stairs, their footsteps ringing out even as they could hear other survivors who were crying openly through the closed doors. When they reached the bottom floor, Jackson opened the door to the basement level and tiptoed to the conference room. There, he cracked the door and peeked in cautiously, expecting the cyborg to be lying supine on the floor the way he'd left it. However, it was standing at attention, not moving at all. Its eyes were glowing red, but the light had faded as if it were incapable of generating that much energy. But it was obviously now a threat.

———————

Jackson backed down the hall, Nadine right behind him. Then they sprinted for the stairs and ran up and up and up until they had, again, reached their fifth-floor suite. Nadine spun Jackson around when they were inside.

"How will we get it out of there?" she fretted.

"I don't know," he replied, still reeling. How *would* they get it out of there? He didn't want anyone to get hurt before they had deactivated or destroyed it. Then he realized their voices were raised slightly, and he worried about giving themselves away, although it was very clear that people were hiding in the building regardless.

"We have to hurry," Nadine urged him.

"How? First, I need to know how to do it without either of us getting hurt," he reminded her, although probably unnecessarily. Surely, she knew that, but she was simply expressing her impatience. He regretted his tone, but he was only expressing his concern for her. However, her expression showed he'd hurt her.

"Look, it's not that I don't appreciate your position. I understand the urgency. I agree with you. I just don't want you to be hurt because I did something stupid without thinking it through. Okay? That's all I meant." He tried to explain, but he wasn't sure she would feel any better after he'd spoken. The words were wrong somehow. But he didn't think he could make any more sense in a few moments of distress when he had more pressing matters to think about than whether he'd upset her. But she was important to him, too. He had to remind himself, and her feelings *did* matter.

She was pacing the room, and he was unaware if it was because of the effect of his words or if she was pondering a way out of the mess they were in. Maybe she even had a solution in mind if he could learn to listen to her more often instead of constantly arguing. It was a wonder that she cared for him at all, he thought. Why was that? Because he was one of the only few men left on Earth? Hopefully, that wasn't the case. He didn't want to be a last resort. Sitting down on the sofa, he patted the space next to him so that she would join him.

"What do you think? How can we get it out before it finishes powering up and kills everyone?" he asked her, forcing his voice to sound more even and calm than he felt. Inside, he felt near panic, thinking that the thing was still inside the hotel as they debated surely futile options.

"Do you think it would follow us if we led it out?" she asked, looking just as terrified of the suggestion as he felt about it.

"It probably would, but how would we get outside without being torn apart like that poor man we saw earlier? And then we would want to get back inside without it following us back in, wouldn't we?" He fell back against the cushions, rubbing the fatigue out of his eyes.

She sighed deeply, then leaned against his shoulder. That was a good sign. So, hopefully, she wasn't mad at him. "We can try to get some of the other people in the hotel to help us," she suggested eventually.

"They could die. I'm not sure it's—no, they could die if we leave it here. Of course, it's worth the risk," he corrected himself. "I just don't know that I can ask anyone else to do that. It would have to be me luring it out."

"But how would you get back in?" she asked him.

"I'm not sure."

"And what if you got attacked by the other cyborgs outside?"

"That was why I didn't want to use the luring plan, to begin with. I'm not sure. Maybe there's something else we haven't thought of." He tried not to think the cyborg was attacking and killing people even as they sat trying to think of a plan.

"Maybe we should just warn everyone to stay away from the basement for now," she thought aloud. "We have to tell them it's there."

"Yeah. I know. That's the least we could do." Putting an arm around Nadine, he tried not to feel sorry for himself, but that was exactly how he felt. "It's my fault," he added. "I brought it here."

"It doesn't matter how it got here, only that it's here," she pointed out.

"Okay. Let's go warn everyone. Maybe some of them have an idea." He patted his legs with finality as if he could summon the courage to admit he had failed them. She nodded acceptance of his plan, such as it was, and they left the suite. They ran down the stairs, knocking on doors, each of them splitting up to cover more ground, warning the others to stay away from the basement for now while they tried to think of what to do. By the time they reached the first floor, they were exhausted and breathing heavily. Nadine knocked on the door to the room Mayra had taken while Jackson left to search the rest of the hotel for stragglers.

"Stay away from the basement. One of those metal skeletons is down there," Nadine warned Mayra urgently. Then, she turned to help Jackson, who was already gone.

"What about my children?" Mayra stopped Nadine before she could depart.

"What do you mean?" Nadine asked skeptically.

"They're somewhere in the hotel. I let them go out to play so they would stop screaming," Mayra admitted.

Jackson, who had returned upon hearing Mayra's raised voice, thought that was the stupidest thing he had ever heard. There were murderous alien creatures lurking about, but she'd let her children roam free as if there were no threat at all. "What did you say?" he nearly shouted at her.

Mayra recoiled, looking like she might have wanted to cry. Surely, she realized her mistake already. However, he doubted she realized all of them. He knew it was her fault that the cyborgs were surrounding the hotel. Her invitation to her relatives and friends had drawn attention to it, and now the cyborgs had realized survivors were hiding inside. Angrily, he spun from Mayra's vicinity and ran toward the lobby, hoping the children were nearby. However, he couldn't see them anywhere. Mayra and Nadine followed him, calling to the boy and girl (Juan and Alicia) as they searched through the other rooms. Jackson's flashlight was the only illumination as they searched the ground floor before they finally guessed that the children must have gone down to the lower level. They hadn't seen the children while they'd been on the upper floors, so there was nowhere else they could have gone.

Jackson returned to the stairwell and cautiously crept down the steps, opening the door when he had reached the basement and peeking out. The little toddlers were in the hallway, running up and down the carpeted path over and over. "Come here," he called to them with false cheer, hoping not to panic them. "Your mother has been looking for you."

They ran toward him, but the door to the ballroom opened at that moment. He wasn't sure if it had been his voice that had attracted it or if it had been the children's playing, but his eyes widened with fear as he saw the cyborg march toward them. The children reached the stairwell, and both Jackson and Mayra swept them up and sprinted up toward the first floor. Would it follow them? Most likely. But what could they do to keep it away from the others?

———————

CHAPTER TEN

They emerged into the lobby from the stairs, and then Jackson ordered Mayra to take the children into her room and barricade the door. Looking around for inspiration, Jackson saw nothing. Their own route out of the hotel was blocked by furniture. Even if they knew they could get back inside, it would take too long to move everything before they could lure the cyborg outside.

They could hear the metallic footsteps tromping up the stairs near the elevators, but they didn't have time to do anything but run. Unable to make it to the fifth floor in time, they hurried into the kitchen, the nearest room where there was any place to hide that wasn't off the stairwell, and then found the large industrial refrigerator. They wouldn't be able to hide for days, but it would do for the short term. They opened the door and closed it behind them, hoping they would be able to get it open again. Then, listening for sounds outside the kitchen, they could make out the cyborg moving through the rooms on the first floor.

Nadine looked at Jackson right before he doused the light as if to say, "We have to do something," but he was out of ideas. They'd even blocked the back door to the massive hotel days earlier. There was no way out of the building that he could think of to lead the dangerous cyborg out and away from the survivors. And Jackson didn't exactly want to run outside amid thousands more of the cyborgs in front of and behind the hotel to do so, either. Doing his best to slow his breathing, he leaned close to the door, hoping he could tell when it was safe to come out. However, the door was heavy steel, and he doubted very much sound could penetrate it.

He feared what the cyborg would do, that it might kill

everyone there. Its footsteps sounded on the tile floor outside, possibly far away, but also possibly in the same room with them. They couldn't be sure through the door. It paced around, searching. Or maybe it was trying to decide what to do. Then, they heard crashing noises as various objects collided with the tiles. What was it doing? Then, fear filled Jackson as he realized it was removing the barricades. The other cyborgs would get inside the hotel. Everyone would die.

"We have to hide," he whispered, his voice shaky. "Whatever happens, we have to stay here."

In the gloom, he couldn't see her reaction, but he sensed her movement as if she might have nodded. He didn't want to chance turning on the light. He wanted to warn the others, but he didn't know how. If he left the refrigerator, he would die, and so would Nadine. He couldn't allow that to happen. But he also felt he couldn't live with himself if he didn't try. The problem was that anything he did would call attention to himself and his hiding place. There wasn't any way he could reach the other survivors. There just wasn't.

Helplessly, he heard several other cyborgs enter the hotel. Knowing there wasn't a guarantee that he and Nadine wouldn't be found where they hid anyway, he listened as several of them walked past the kitchen. Then, one paused at the entrance as if unsure. It walked inside the room, surveying it, and then it began opening the cabinets. When the screams started, Jackson wasn't sure if the cyborg was still there. He couldn't hear over the terrified and anguished sounds of the dying. He gripped Nadine tightly, feeling like part of himself was dying too like he had failed in every way imaginable. Angry tears streaked down his face as he thought of all the deaths he'd failed to prevent.

And he waited. And waited. He knew they were dead. Their hiding place wasn't that secure. It wasn't barricaded and hidden. The door even opened the wrong way, so he couldn't hold it closed, as if his strength would really be enough against one of the metallic monsters out there dismembering innocent people. Mayra's family had managed to survive the first assault, but they were dead now because of Jackson himself, he thought. But the door remained closed, and he could still hear screams in the hallways, loud, as if they were in the room with him. It was horrific.

Hours passed. It must have been. When they could no longer hear the screams, they could still hear the pounding of the metallic legs striking the tiles as the cyborgs searched from room to room. There weren't hundreds of them, but there didn't need to be. There only needed to be one. Even when everything fell silent hours later, he and Nadine didn't emerge. They stayed in the refrigerator, worrying that they would die from oxygen deprivation and that they wouldn't be able to get the door open when the time came. But how would they know it was safe to leave? They listened and listened. Nothing.

In the darkness, they waited, clinging to each other as if that might make a difference. Nadine didn't make a sound. Normally, she might have cried out as the massacre started, but she let Jackson calm her, and she only shivered and shivered, waiting for it to be over. But when would it be over? Would the cyborgs leave the hotel? Were they posted in the hallways, waiting for survivors to emerge from unknown hiding places? Or had they assumed they had killed everyone, and they were now outside roaming the countryside again?

Eventually, Jackson felt his breathing become more labored. The space felt sweltering and hot, and he knew it wasn't a warm day. Every breath felt like he was underwater. It sapped his energy, and he wanted to sleep. The urge was almost overwhelming, just to rest and wait some more. But he knew he would never wake again if he did. They had to leave. He cautiously opened the door, feeling the oxygen seep into the crack as he pressed his eye to it to see if anyone was in the room. The kitchen appeared empty, but he had to admit his vision was limited. There was a large kitchen island blocking his view.

However, he was afraid to turn on the flashlight to be sure. He only knew the cyborg's eyes lit up, and he could spot them from far away. There was nothing that looked like a light outside the refrigerator, but anything further from him he couldn't see. His eyes tried to adjust to the gloom, but there wasn't a hint of red light anywhere. He crept from the space, kneeling down to keep behind the island, while Nadine followed him. Partially, he wished she'd stay behind and be safe, but he wasn't sure there was any place truly safe at all anyway.

Carefully, he placed his feet on the floor one by one and made his way across to the kitchen doorway. He couldn't see any red lights indicating cyborgs were nearby when he crept out to the corridor, but the light flooding in from the now unblocked main entrance told a story of horror and destruction. The floor was bathed in blood, as some of the cyborgs must have killed some of the survivors as they'd attempted to flee the hotel. Jackson wanted to leave, wanted to get out of the stench and horrific memories, but he wasn't sure it was safe to do so. He tried to peek out the door, but there he could see an army waiting for him. Hoping they couldn't see him, he gestured for Nadine to help him rebuild the barricades. They worked quickly to push the furniture back up against the door, hopefully not blocking their own escape.

But why were the cyborgs still there? Did they know there were still survivors in the hotel? How many had made it? Or were Jackson and Nadine the only ones? Grief almost overwhelmed him as he hurried to Mayra's room, hoping Alicia and Juan had survived at the very least. However, when he got there, it was obvious they had not. The door was open, and red had spattered on the white paint. He didn't look any closer. The cyborgs didn't care that Juan and Alicia had only been children, not even old enough to pose any kind of threat. They couldn't survive on their own, but the cyborgs had killed them as if they could have saved the entire planet.

Turning away, he headed for the stairwell, still anxious, thinking cyborgs might be hiding somewhere. The doors were open on all the floors, bloody and covered in various bodily fluids and offal as Jackson passed. Nadine whimpered as she followed him. He wanted to reassure her, but he was just as disgusted as she was, maybe even more so. But he wasn't disgusted by the sights he saw in the hotel as much as he was with himself for bringing the supposedly dead cyborg, the Trojan horse, into the hotel to begin with. It was his fault. All of it. All of the deaths were on him.

Reaching the fifth-floor suite, they saw that the door was open.

strangely pristine in the rest of the building. They searched each room on the floor as they had done on the lower ones, then they returned to the relative safety of the suite, closing and barricading the door as if it could really protect them as if it could keep out the negative thoughts infecting Jackson's mind like a virus. He couldn't shake the feelings of guilt, the remorse.

Nadine seemed to sense some of it. She didn't say a word. But when he collapsed onto the sofa and broke down, she put her arms around him as if to comfort him the way he had done for her during the siege. It felt warm and inviting and far too affectionate. He didn't deserve it, he felt. Standing suddenly, he let out a loud bellowing scream, releasing pent-up feelings of primal rage and frustration as if he could somehow bring back the lives that had been lost. But when he finally calmed enough to look, he saw fear on Nadine's face, and he wished he'd been able to control his feelings better. He collapsed again, leaning against her and weeping.

"I'm so sorry, Nadine," he cried.

She held him again, but wary this time, as if thinking he would explode again, as before. "What are you sorry for?" she asked quietly. "For being upset by what happened? I am, too."

"You were right. You were so right. I should have listened to you," he continued as if he hadn't heard anything she had said.

"When?" she asked, pausing and leaning back so that she could see his face. The light rested in front of them on the coffee table, facing upward so that it flooded the room with its feebly warm glow.

"I insisted we bring it along. Stupid. So stupid. I should have listened to you," he rambled on.

"It was dead. How could you have known it would do that?"

He looked at her as if he could finally face her disappointment. "*You* knew. You didn't want to bring it, and I did. So, we brought it because I never listen to you." Bitterness colored his tone, and he tried to make her understand that his anger wasn't directed at her. How could he blame her when all she had done was try to protect him? But he should have known. He should have *known*.

Her eyes were fierce as she replied. "Stop it. Stop it now. You didn't kill those people. You didn't bring it here so that it would let them in. You didn't even know it would wake and do anything at all. Those cyborgs did all of it. You didn't make them do anything."

So, she wasn't disappointed in him at all. That almost hurt more than if she had been. The disappointment he would have understood. The compassion was something else. It stung. He wiped his eyes furiously, then lay back, groaning as he took a deep breath to steady his thoughts. It wouldn't do him any good not to listen to her. He should have learned that by now. She was right. She had to be right.

"Okay. You're right. You're always right," he conceded.

Instead of being happy, though, she looked angry. "I'm not always right. Stop that. Stop feeling sorry for yourself and help me. We need to get out of here eventually. What are we going to do?"

He shook his head. "You shouldn't ask. I'll probably just get us both killed."

She threw a sofa cushion at him and stalked away, closing the door to the bedroom in anger. He wanted to follow, but he was in no state to have a conversation, especially not an intelligent one. Depression was clouding his mind, and he couldn't shake it off. What if they were doomed anyway? What if there was nothing that they could do to stop the cyborgs, regardless? He wanted to flee, to find some far-off island that the cyborgs had never found and hide there. But that was just as unrealistic as trying to fight them.

Taking several deep breaths, he then wiped the fatigue out of his eyes. It wasn't helping. They had hardly slept since all of the drama had begun a few days earlier. He wanted their old lives back, living in the cottage on the beach. It wasn't a lot to ask, he didn't think. They just wanted to be left alone. Sometimes they'd traded with the neighbors, the few people they could find that had decided to settle in the area. But mostly, it was just him and Nadine. And now, he feared he'd scared her or angered her enough that she might leave him. Of course, that was the last thing he wanted.

He stood and entered the small kitchen, finding two plates and assembling a few of their foods into a meager meal for two. Before entering the bedroom, however, he knocked lightly on the door. Although he didn't hear a response, he opened it slowly, almost as if waiting for her to hurl something else at him. She didn't. She lay facing away from him on the bed, her back like an icy wall between them.

Setting the light and the plate on the nightstand, he sat down on the mattress next to her. "I'm sure you can understand why I'm so upset. I shouldn't have taken out my frustrations on you, though, and I *should* listen to you more

THE BLOOD HOTEL 133

often. But I know I'm being foolish to assume I have all the answers or that everything is my fault. It's not. But this is traumatic, okay? We're both going to mess up sometimes. I know I did today or whenever I brought that thing in here. But you're right that I didn't make any of that happen. Can we just, please, not lose each other simply because I was scared and angry that those people died? I can't lose you. I can't."

Flipping over to face him, she sighed. "I don't blame you. I know you, though And you may think you make more mistakes than I do, but you're wrong. I listen to you because when we both work together, things are okay. That's all I want. I don't want to be the one person making decisions because it works better when it's both of us. I want to stop the cyborgs, but I want to survive the assault, too. I don't want to lose you either, despite what you might think."

Part of him wanted to smile, but his depression was too great. He only managed a weak smirk. "Thanks. I'm glad we can both agree on that, at least."

"We agree a lot of the time. Don't do that, either."

"Okay, okay. Sorry. Just feeling a bit down. Forgive my inability to see clearly right now. Maybe we should just... wait. Those cyborgs were *waiting*. How did they know how many survivors were in the hotel? Do they know we're still here?" He felt like his mind was trying to make sense of something, but the answer was still elusive.

"I don't know. Maybe they just saw the room was empty, and it was obviously occupied, so they deduced there were other people somewhere else in the hotel."

"Yeah, but we could have been in one of the other rooms, or the children could have been playing up here or any number of other scenarios. They're still here en masse. How do they know there's *still* someone here?" He stood and walked back out to the living room, then he peeked around the barricade in front of the window, curling back a small portion of the curtain so that he could see the grounds surrounding the hotel below. Thousands and thousands of cyborgs lined the parking lot and the road in front of the building. Their eyes lit up the ground like evil crimson stars.

All he could do was stare. The sun was somehow only setting then (or it was the next day and setting again), and he wondered how long the cyborgs would wait. Would they wait days? Weeks? Months? He worried about how he and Nadine could get food when they ran out. And he didn't want to wait until then to stop them. More people would die if he didn't find a way.

Nadine waited patiently behind him, and he turned to face her, dismay registering in his expression. "There are thousands of them. Thousands. We'll never get out."

He could tell it wasn't what she wanted to hear. She wanted to hear the cyborgs had a weakness. And really, he did, too. He wanted to find it almost more than she did. Despite what she said, he felt responsible for the deaths, and he wanted to prevent more if he could. Pacing in front of the window, he tried to figure out what he was missing. There had to be something.

"They're everywhere?" she asked, seeming like she already knew the answer.

"Yes. I don't see a break anywhere, but I can't see behind us. I doubt they'd neglect one whole side of the building, though."

Defeated, she sat on the sofa again. Jackson retrieved the plate he'd left in the bedroom and brought it to her. "We need to think about this," he insisted, still trying to solve the puzzle. "I don't know if it's important or not, but if they are only guessing someone is here, then maybe they'll leave eventually. If they are sure, then they might wait forever. So, why are they still here?"

She took the plate and began nibbling half-heartedly on the strips of fish. He took a peanut and cracked the shell while he waited for her response. "I don't know what you saw. If you didn't see any kind of opening, then how can we know what their motivations are?"

"Do you think we should wait and see?"

"No. This place is going to smell worse by tomorrow. We'll barely be able to stand it."

He agreed. "So, they probably know that. Maybe they're waiting for us to leave on our own."

Shaking her head, she wasn't sure. "I thought you said they might not know someone is still here. If this is a 'just in case' type of thing, then they still can't be sure, can they? What if we can make it longer than they think? Or what if we're just *that* afraid of leaving?"

He had to admit she had a point. "Okay, so that's not their motivation then." Feeling suddenly very exhausted, he leaned back against the cushions and stared into space. There were cracks in the ceiling, but he had grown so used to that sort of thing that he barely noticed anymore. Everything everywhere was damaged. Even him. How could anyone have gone through everything he'd been through with Nadine unscathed? He had to admit that he was probably not the only one who'd been hurt. Remembering Nadine's early days grieving the loss of her boyfriend, he thought she'd come out stronger in the end. Maybe he would, too. Then again, maybe neither of them had a choice.

————

CHAPTER ELEVEN

Days passed, and the smell of decomposition and death grew ever stronger and stronger. They could hardly breathe. The only thing that tempered their suffering was that the outside temperature began to cool, especially at night, so the smell wasn't as overpowering as it might have been. But that was relative. The odor was so strong that they felt they would never get it out of their clothes or off their skin. Even the floral soaps that Nadine had made could only do so much. It was a distraction. Their main concern was that they would run out of food and water eventually, even as they began to ration what they had to make it last longer.

Periodically, Jackson peered out the corner of the window to check on their malevolent audience, which never seemed to change at all. They stood unmoving as they surrounded the building, only inches between them. He couldn't see a way out at all. If he'd ever wondered what hell was like, he now knew. It was this hotel. The stench alone was enough to make it nearly unbearable. But the possibility of death on exit turned it into a lethal prison.

Eventually, they knew they would have to decide on an end game. Jackson didn't want to be torn apart by the cyborgs, and he didn't want that for Nadine, either. He also didn't want to starve to death. If worse came to worst, he knew he would have to take matters into his own hands or give the horrible responsibility to Nadine. As he didn't want to think about it himself, he didn't want the burden on her, either. But he would have to discuss his last wishes with her at some point, just so they would have a plan in place. They still had several weapons which, although mostly harmless to the cyborgs, would do the job they wanted them to do.

Jackson didn't chance moving about the hotel. He stayed in the room, lying in bed, which smelled of rotten flesh by then, but nowhere else was any better. It wasn't actually the bed, he was sure. It was in the air. But he was sure that if he took a moment to sniff the fabrics he couldn't tell the difference anymore. Maybe the particles had clogged his sinus passages, and he'd never smell anything else ever again. No, wait. That wasn't how it worked. The opposite would be true. Sighing, he rolled over to face Nadine, who barely moved either. She spent most of her time sleeping. He was sure that was because when she was asleep, she wasn't as aware of the smell, but he never asked.

Even eating was a challenge, as hungry as he was. All he could taste was what he perceived as the decaying flesh of the dead below them. Surely, he thought he would be so traumatized from the experience that he'd become fully vegetarian, if not already. The fish was protein, for lack of many other sources. But he couldn't help feeling that the stringy meat tasted like the people he'd met only a few days earlier. He thought of the old movie *Soylent Green* and wished he could get the image out of his mind.

They barely spoke to each other, either. Opening his mouth seemed an unnecessary way to bring more odorous particles in, another way to taste the air that he didn't particularly want to taste. But it was wearing on him. He missed the easy familiarity he'd had with her. He missed the simple conversation, even if she didn't always agree with him. She agreed with him enough, he decided, although he knew he probably didn't realize it most of the time. Now, he wished he'd told her how he'd felt much sooner. He wished he'd complimented her more and been more supportive. Hopefully, it wasn't too late.

In lieu of words, he reached out a hand to stroke her cheek, and her soft smile at his touch warmed him inside. He wished he could find something to say, something that would change their predicament, something that would save their lives. But he had no ideas any longer. Staring out the window had taken those away. So, he lay there, watching Nadine as she sleepily played with his hand. Even intimacy was out of the question. He couldn't even think of such a thing, even as he still saw the faces of those he felt he'd killed, even if he hadn't done so directly. She could obviously sense his melancholy, and she did her best to keep his spirits up. Her gentle squeeze on his hand brought him back to the present, and he realized how distracted he'd felt. It was hard to focus with so little to do.

He returned the squeeze to let her know he was paying attention, then he shifted closer so that she could put her head on his shoulder. "You know we can't stay here," he mumbled, still holding onto her hand.

"We can't leave either." Her voice was slightly muffled, but her lips were close enough to his ear that he could make it out.

"I know that. That's my point, actually." Trying to gain the courage to say what he needed to say, he almost wished he could see into her eyes. Almost. He was afraid of what he would see there, but he didn't feel like having a serious conversation without her being able to see his own expression. It wasn't fair. Sighing in defeat, he gestured for her to sit up. It was unfortunate, as he'd been comfortable, but he didn't think he could, in good conscience, ambush her like that. "We need to make a plan for if we can't make it out. I don't want them to get to us. I know you don't either. I'd rather we decided our own fate."

"The guns? You want us to kill ourselves?"

He shook his head. "Not now. Not ever, if we can help it. But if they breach the building or we can't get food anymore or…whatever. I don't want them to decide what happens to us. You can do what you want, but please promise me you will do whatever it takes to make sure they can't kill us the way they did the others."

Nodding solemnly, she wiped a stray tear away. "Okay."

"Promise me," he repeated.

"I promise," she agreed. However, her expression showed she wasn't happy with his decision.

"I don't plan on giving up just yet, okay? Last resort only. I just want you to know what my wishes are. We'll do our best to get out of this."

Slightly more enthusiastically, she nodded again, understanding.

"Okay," he said, gesturing again as he lay down so she could put her head back on his shoulder. Strangely, she did so, although he hadn't been sure she wasn't too upset. He held her hand and hoped he was being comforting after he'd finally broken the taboo subject with her. It wasn't exactly what he wanted to do either, but he feared the cyborgs more than Nadine or himself.

———

Jackson didn't want to check the window anymore. He was

sure it didn't make a difference, that the cyborgs were still there and, therefore, there was no point. But he checked, anyway, his daily routine, and saw that, indeed, they were still there as expected. What else could they do? How could he and Nadine escape? Frustrated and hungry, he wanted to find a way out soon, but he didn't think that would happen unless the cyborgs either: 1.) made a mistake or 2.) left because they believed the hotel was empty. Probably neither would happen.

He shuffled back to the bedroom and failure, where he lay down next to Nadine again. He was sure he wouldn't be able to bike any more if he didn't keep up his level of fitness. By now, his muscles were becoming weaker, and he could feel it in his level of fatigue. She hardly stirred, and he knew she was as depressed and hopeless as he was. But how could he cheer her up when he understood her feelings so well? Surely, all of their fears were founded. What were the chances of their being able to escape anyway? Very low, if at all.

Part of him felt the need to get up to start exercising again in one way or another, but his motivation was so little that he felt it was impossible. He couldn't even summon the energy to take a shower right at that moment. It hardly mattered. Their soap would run out, and it hardly changed anything anyway, as the foul odor remained even after he'd freshly scrubbed his skin and hair clean. Nothing mattered. Nothing changed. There was only one outcome he felt was inevitable, and that was the one he'd spoken about with Nadine. It wasn't what he wanted. He wanted to go back to the cottage on the beach and live out the rest of his days with her, but he feared that wouldn't happen. In a world where the cyborgs had invaded again, his days wouldn't be restful if he didn't stop them somehow.

But this lake had no dome over it as Smithton Lake had. It had no control center or anything of the sort. Did the cyborgs have any such things anymore? Or was the beacon the cyborgs had set up on the first day performing the same function? Perhaps they were all unrelated, and then what could he do? If he destroyed the beacon and everything remained the same, then he really didn't know what to do.

And how would he do anything at all, trapped inside that tragic and wretched hotel? He'd tried to destroy the beacon once before and failed. What could make him think he might be able to succeed if he tried again? What weapon could he possibly use? He had nothing new. The cyborgs were the ones with the advantage. They had all the technology. And then it clicked. He'd find a way to use their own technology against them. If he lived, anyway. He didn't yet have a plan. They had to escape the hotel first and find something they could use, but it was a start. It was hope. It was motivation.

He stood and returned to the living room, returned to the damned window that never showed anything new. Then, he peeked out through the same crack he always used, hoping the cyborgs' eyesight wasn't good enough to spot him looking out at them. Determined now, he stared and waited. He wasn't just checking to see if they were there. He was analyzing them for patterns. But they had no patterns. They stood immobile and indifferent. Their only goal was to kill all of the humans so they could have a planet all to themselves. Jackson had tried to reason with them five years earlier, but they were cold and remorseless. But there had to be a weakness somewhere.

There had to be. One day they would move.

Nadine remained behind in the bedroom. Maybe she cared what he did. Maybe she didn't. He wasn't sure. If he were her, he probably wouldn't have the energy to figure him out either. But he watched and watched, staring out the window at the sea of red eyes. If it took several days longer, he would find it. He would be there to spot whatever mistake they made. They weren't perfect. There was no such thing.

Then, just when he was about to give up to finally go take the shower he desperately needed, he heard something that made his blood freeze through. A human voice calling from outside the hotel. "Come out, and you will not be harmed!"

———

He seriously doubted the veracity of the words. Of course, he'd seen what had happened to the others. He knew the cyborgs had no mercy. Looking around, he finally saw what he'd heard. There was a human collaborator standing at the front of the crowd, holding some sort of device to project his voice that he must have borrowed from the cyborgs. Jackson had no desire to speak to the man as there was nothing the man could say to persuade him that he told the truth. Anything Jackson did to engage with the collaborator would be a mistake. The man's words would seep into him like poison and would weaken his resolve. He couldn't listen.

Nadine approached him then, standing in the doorway to the bedroom, looking terrified. "No. We're not leaving. We can't," he told her, hoping to alleviate some of her fear. "I don't believe him, and I know you don't either."

She shook her head, and he walked over to put an arm

around her. "Who is it? They don't talk. Who is talking?" she asked.

"A man is standing there with them. He's speaking for them."

"Why would he do that?" Her voice broke slightly as if she couldn't believe anyone could ever be a traitor to their own people, even though it had happened throughout history.

"He probably believes he'll be saved if he cooperates," Jackson explained, although he knew she understood the concept. She wasn't asking literally. She probably meant that she couldn't comprehend the man's decision.

Her expression showed his answer was unnecessary. "I know that, but why? Still. Why? I wouldn't do it, and neither would you. Why would this horrible man do such a thing?"

"I don't know," Jackson corrected himself. "That I'll never understand."

"He'll watch us die just to save himself. I hope it haunts him the rest of his life."

He squeezed her shoulder reassuringly, unable to say anything else that hadn't been said. Part of him didn't want to admit the obvious, that the man probably wouldn't live very much longer. When he'd outlived his usefulness, he would be killed like the rest of them.

The voice sounded again. "If you come out peacefully, you will not be harmed! You have my word!"

"Yeah, for whatever that's worth," Jackson commented drily. He went back to the window, letting go of Nadine so that he could push the curtain aside by an inch to press his eye to the gap. He didn't want the cyborgs to know which room was occupied, although it wasn't really a difficult guess.

From five floors up, Jackson could still make out the man's posture and expressions to some degree. The man appeared confident as if he truly believed he would be safe if he cooperated. He *trusted* the cyborgs. Well, that was definitely a mistake, Jackson thought. He wished he could convince the man to leave so that he could save at least one life, but he doubted the man would believe him. Even so, he had to try, didn't he? But if he went downstairs to talk, he would have to brave the stench of death even stronger than what they could smell from the fifth floor with their doors closed and blocked. It would be unbearable. But that wasn't enough of a reason to allow the man to die, was it? Of course not. He tried to gain the courage to face the downstairs floors, but he found himself dreading what he would experience. It had been horrific the first time he'd run through. It would be worse now.

When he turned from the window and headed for the door, Nadine looked alarmed. "You're not going to leave me, are you?" she asked, frightened.

"No. I'm going to try to get that man to see reason and come inside," he corrected her.

She didn't look pleased. "He'll betray us like the cyborg did."

"So, I should just let them kill him, then?" he argued.

"Better him than us," she said stubbornly.

"What if I can save his life?" His voice sounded more plaintive than he would have liked, a bit weak and almost sad. It wasn't the confident tone he'd tried to convey.

"It wasn't your fault," she reminded him. "You have

nothing to pay for."

He loved that she realized what he was doing and that she still didn't blame him for what happened. "Maybe not. But this man's life is worth saving. I have to try something. If he doesn't listen, I'll come right back."

"I'm coming with you," she argued.

That gave him pause. Risking his own safety was one thing, but risking hers was another thing entirely. "No, you're not. You're going to stay here."

She didn't say another word, but she glared at him stubbornly until he waved his hand in acquiescence. Then, they stepped out into the hallway, where the smell hit them like a ton of bricks. It only increased in intensity as they made their way down the stairs and to the lobby, where the red smears had turned brownish and were covered in flies that had somehow gotten into the building. He felt his stomach lurch, but he managed to keep everything down as he approached a window and moved a chair to see out.

"Come out on your own, and you will not be harmed!" the collaborator called out, looking directly at the front door, where he seemed to expect them to appear.

Jackson waved his hand for the man to approach, hoping to get him far enough away from the cyborgs that he might reconsider an alliance. The cyborgs were hopefully too far away to see him clearly. The man was standing to the front but several feet away from the door. Seeing Jackson's signal, he walked toward the window, taking several minutes to get close enough that they could communicate.

"If you come out, they will not hurt you," he said to the glass.

Jackson shook his head. "I'm trying to save your life. They'll kill you when you're not useful to them anymore. You should come inside with us."

"No. They won't harm me if I help them," the man disagreed, but a seed of doubt had been planted. He appeared slightly troubled.

"Are you sure? They're not human. They want us dead. I've talked to them. They want this planet empty of life save for themselves. The entire world, just for them. That's what they told me. They don't want to share. I asked."

The man looked over his shoulder at the malevolent skeleton-like cyborgs that were lining the parking lot and the field beyond, up to the lakeshore. Then, he turned back to Jackson. "You must come out. They won't hurt you if you come out!"

"Help us, then. If you won't come inside, will you lure them away? We can stop them, but we need help," Jackson begged.

The man lowered his voice almost to a whisper, loud enough to hear through the glass, "I can't help you. Sorry." Then, he backed away from the window as if he hadn't said a word. He continued to use the device in his hand, a small cylinder with a grate on one side, to call out to the surrounding area and the upper floors of the hotel, asking for their surrender.

Jackson, puzzled by the man's behavior, pushed the chair back into position, then ran with Nadine back up the stairs and to the fifth floor. They closed the door, taking deep breaths as they came into contact with the slightly cleaner air.

"What was that about?" Nadine asked.

"Was he pretending he hadn't talked to us? Is he trying to help us?" Jackson wondered aloud.

"Is he crazy?" Nadine suggested.

He conceded that she might be right. "I don't know." Then, changing the topic, "If we go down again, we need scarves or something to cover our faces. That was horrific."

"Agreed," she said, coughing to clear her airway.

At first, he thought she might actually throw up, but she seemed to calm enough after she took several deep breaths. "Okay, I'm going to rinse off," he informed her, heading for the shower.

But she went to the window he always used to look out and peered around the curtain. He paused to wait for her report, and she turned to face him with astonishment. "They're leaving!"

Jackson ran to join her and pushed the curtain only slightly to one side so that he could see out. Indeed, the cyborgs were slowly walking in one direction, heading away from the lake. "Get our things together. When they're gone, we'll leave. Just in case they come back, I want to be gone before that happens."

Nadine nodded, then they raced around the space, gathering everything that had been removed from their bags and repacking the suitcases. Carefully, they packed the food, then they wrapped their old garments that had been washed in the bathroom sink around their mouths and noses to help keep out the odors from downstairs. Returning to the window, he peeked out and saw that the countryside was empty of cyborgs. He looked at Nadine and nodded, then they ran to the door and down the stairs to where they'd left their bikes in the lobby. They stowed their bags in their trailers, then they walked over to the window where they'd talked to the captive man. Nothing. There was nothing.

They moved the furniture as silently as they could, unblocking the door, then pedaled their bikes out into the fresh air. Trying not to make a sound even as they coughed the foul air out of their lungs, they quickly sped away from the hotel and down the road, opposite to the direction the cyborgs had been walking, circling back toward the beach cottage. But they had a stop to make first.

———————

CHAPTER
TWELVE

"Did that man lead them away?" Nadine asked Jackson, pulling the t-shirt down from over her mouth so that he could hear her.

"I don't know. I don't want to assume. He said he couldn't help us. I don't know what happened," he replied, copying her actions.

She pedaled hard to put some distance between them and the nightmare hotel. He had a hard time keeping up with her. As fatigued and unmotivated as he'd been for the previous several days, his muscles had atrophied. Also, he had to remind himself that he wasn't as young as she was, and he couldn't bounce back as quickly. He was soon out of breath and struggling before they'd gone more than a few miles, and he wasn't sure he wouldn't just pass out.

Becoming lightheaded as they rounded a curve, he felt himself start to tumble off the bike before he could stop it, and he crashed onto the road in a heap. The sound was enough to catch Nadine's attention, and she skidded to a stop before resting her bike and running over to help him back to his feet.

"Are you okay?" she asked, trying to support his weight as he struggled to stand.

"I don't know. I think so," he responded, although he was definitely unsure. He mounted the bike again and nodded to her to continue.

Obviously reluctantly, she returned to her bike and began to pedal down the road again, but more slowly this time, and her eyes frequently flicked over to him to be sure he was still there as she rode. It was as if she were afraid that he would drop dead on the concrete. And he actually wasn't completely convinced that it wasn't a possibility either.

Fearing a heart attack, he scanned the area for someplace to stop and rest, although they hadn't gone far enough from the hotel for comfort. They'd cleared the area around Overton Lake, however, and they were in the forested countryside, still surrounded by mountains. The lake had already receded behind them, but they watched for signs that they were nearing another town.

By the time they found another crumbling road sign indicating the distance to the next stop, they had already realized it would be quite a long way by stopping briefly to consult the map. If they continued on that road, they would find a junction that would take them back the way they wanted to go. Even so, he was unsure he was making the right decision, and he almost hoped Nadine would have talked him out of it. However, she had agreed, so they were heading for the last place they'd seen one of the spaceships. Although there was a possibility there would still be cyborgs in the vicinity, they hoped to gain entry and find something they could use to fight them or destroy them. If they were lucky, it would be temporarily abandoned. If they were not... well, they would worry about that later.

Seeing the long, unbroken line on the map, he wasn't sure he could make it that far, however. But he didn't dare sleep outdoors. It wasn't safe. "I need a minute," he wheezed as he came to a stop.

Nadine's bike stopped ahead of his. She glanced back over her shoulder, still apparently worried about being followed. But she eventually nodded. Leaning back in the seat, she took a long gulp of water from her bottle as she glanced around them as if cyborgs or some other enemy would pounce out at them.

Jackson's face was red as he tried to breathe, then he chugged down more water than he probably should have, hoping it was just mild dehydration. He knew it wasn't, though. He was out of shape, and he knew it. The lack of exercise had made more than just his arms and legs weaker, but his heart as well. It was a major mistake that the depression had made him commit, but it was really too late to correct it at that point. Gasping, he wiped the sweat from his forehead with the back of his hand, still hoping to get going shortly. Nadine's face was concerned, though. Perhaps he looked worse off than he realized.

"I'll be okay," he lied. "Just needed a second. We can continue."

"Are you sure?" she asked, obviously not believing him.

"Yes. I'm fine. Let's go." He fought to go up the incline, cresting it and then heading down before she followed him as if she were unsure that he would make it all the way up.

He coasted down, not daring to go full speed and risk a collision or worse. Then, when they were both side by side again, he picked up his speed a little to make up some lost time. Neither of them wanted to be out at night where they wouldn't be able to see without a light which would guide any enemies to them like the beacon they wanted to destroy.

They rode without speaking for several more miles, with her glancing over frequently to be sure he wasn't about to collapse again. However, the air had cooled, and he didn't feel as winded once they'd gotten further from the deathtrap as he thought of it. The air was clean, and there was a breeze that ruffled his hair, making him feel almost as if the hotel was in the distant past. It wouldn't soon be forgotten, however. He still dreamed of the massacre every night. How had Nadine gotten through those first few nights after David's murder without going crazy, he wondered? She'd been shy and terrified, sure. But she was still there with him even after all the intervening years.

When he saw the town, at first, he thought he might be hallucinating, a strange mirage appearing before him. But then, he could see streets and buildings and a big ground-level billboard that read, "Welcome to Strathmore!" right as they entered the city limits. The billboard was barely legible, and some weeds had torn off the H, but it was almost as if the weeds had respected what came before and took over the previous form as a leaf came across two stalks right at the same place the crossbar of the H had once been. He wanted to stop, desperately wanted to stop. However, he didn't trust his own judgment anymore.

"What do you think?" he asked. "Should we stop?"

Taking one look at him, she nodded emphatically. "Yes. You won't make it much farther."

Was there an implied insult, or was she just concerned? Perhaps he shouldn't try to read so much into a simple comment, he thought. He rode toward a side street and then looked for anything that looked secure but inconspicuous. They both rode around the town for a few minutes, not wanting to be stuck in the same situation as before. However, Jackson was aware that they had been fine until Mayra had invited her entourage to come to stay with them. So, perhaps it wasn't the location that was to blame. Blaming Mayra for the disaster wasn't in him either, though.

When he saw the building, it seemed perfect. It was a small granite-faced building, a jewelry store with an apartment above it. The jewelry store had secure doors and few windows, only window displays on the exterior, which had been cleared out by thieves, although for some unknown purpose. Jewelry held no value anymore. They entered through the back, bringing the bikes into the store, and then they used the furniture from the office to block the doors. The stairs in the rear of the store led up one level to where the one-bedroom apartment waited for them. Using the flashlight, Jackson picked the lock to the front door, then cautiously opened it, expecting someone to be there waiting for him with a weapon raised. But it was obvious the place was deserted. Everything looked pristine but with a layer of dust over it.

Regardless, he searched the rooms and then blocked up the front door with Nadine's help once they were sure it was empty. Then, they went about cleaning up some of the surfaces and making the bed so that they could get some much-needed rest. He wanted to go straight to sleep, but she made him eat dinner, such as they had remaining before he finally got up to take a long shower and collapse into the blankets. Unaware of whether she lay next to him or whether she took the opportunity to shower as well, he could feel sleep tugging at the last layers of his consciousness before he was whisked into a dream where he was trying to escape a strange hotel with no exits and only endless darkened corridors.

Golden rays of sunshine crept through a crack in their barricade, drilling into his eyes and waking him. He turned over, rubbing them to get the dark spots out of his vision, then he opened them to see that Nadine was sitting there nibbling on some dried berries. She held the bowl out to him when he saw her, and he grunted as he tried to sit up, his whole body sore.

"You need a hot bath," she said as he took a handful of berries from the bowl.

He only grunted again as if he were incapable of speech just then.

"I'll join you," she added, winking as if there really were any hot water anywhere.

And he laughed, unable to restrain himself. Pure joy was in her expression as she grinned at his amusement, so he couldn't help but feel overwhelmed. Leaning forward, he kissed her, tasting the red berries on her lips. They were sweet with a hint of tartness that was very pleasant as he pressed his own lips to hers. She giggled as he nearly tumbled over onto the bed, spilling the berries. Apparently, he still didn't have his equilibrium back.

Sitting back, he tried to recover some of the lost fruit, but he was laughing lightly as he did so, plopping one into his or her mouth periodically as often as he placed them back in the bowl.

"Okay, so I'm not a gymnast," he commented, chewing a berry.

Her giggling increased. "Obviously."

He gave her a wry grin. "Thanks for the encouragement."

"I'm not dating you for your flexibility," she laughed.

"We're dating?" he asked.

"Well, we can't exactly get married, though." She

looked slightly rueful.

"You want to get married already?" He looked at her incredulously as if she had suggested they fly to outer space instead.

"What do you mean 'already'? It's been five years that we've known each other," she reminded him.

Clearing his throat as he tried to think of an answer, he simply sat there staring at her, his mouth agape. "Yeah, but we weren't...erm...you know...dating then."

"Having sex, you mean?" she corrected him with a mischievous grin.

"Okay, yes."

"Does that matter, though?" she asked.

He thought about it. *Did* it matter? Probably not, in the grand scheme of things. "Okay. You want to get married?"

"Wow. So romantic. I'm touched," she teased him.

He shrugged and then winked. "So. What do you think?"

Suddenly, it was her turn to be surprised. "Really?" she asked.

"You asked first. But you said we can't do anything about it. Why not? Without a government agency overseeing that sort of thing, we can do it ourselves. Who can say we're not married if we want to be?"

She smiled, reassured. "Okay. Let's do that. But I still want a ceremony of sorts if we can manage it."

"We'll stand under the trees and make vows to each other. I'll make you a ring," he promised.

Then, her berry-stained lips were on his again, and she was the one to knock over the bowl.

———

He wanted to keep going on their quest, but his body was still recovering from the ride to get there. His legs ached, and his back felt tight. The hot bath Nadine had suggested sounded wonderful, but he wondered how they would ever heat up enough water without his fire pit in the back yard of their little cottage. He missed home. But there was no way they could go back until they'd destroyed the cyborgs, however they managed that. They had to use the cyborgs' technology against them as the cyborgs were the only ones who had any sort of weapons or communication devices. There had to be a way to stop them as before.

But that day, all he could do was sleep. It had been too long with the nightmares for him to feel rested, so he lay in the bed feeling wiped out and sore. Nadine seemed to be fine, as she disappeared from time to time as if other duties were keeping her busy. Perhaps she'd boiled some more water. Perhaps she'd done some laundry. He had no idea what she was actually doing, and he didn't have the energy to actually ask her. Instead, he let his body tell him what it needed, and he slept and slept.

When he finally woke feeling somewhat more alert, she was drying her hair with a towel as if she'd just bathed or showered. As she was shivering slightly, it was clear the water was very cold, and he debated whether he wanted to take one himself or not. Unfortunately, he still felt like the death odor was on him, whether it was really there or not, and he felt like scrubbing his skin until it finally smelled clean.

"How long was I asleep?" he asked as he sat up, hoping to keep from falling asleep again by changing his position.

"In hours or days?" she responded.

"Days?" he couldn't help but blurt out.

"Two." She didn't sound upset, so maybe she knew he had been incapable of staying awake.

"Thanks." He groaned slightly as he moved, feeling his bones pop into place as he shifted to stand up. Then, he stood there debating again how badly he wanted to be clean. Pretty badly, he decided. He headed for the bathroom.

Once the water touched him, he could hardly keep from shivering himself. It felt like ice. But he forced himself to use Nadine's soap and to scrub himself as thoroughly as he could before practically leaping out of the tub and drying himself with a ragged towel which had obviously seen better days. It was a cotton blend, so it was hanging together better than a solely cotton towel would have by then, but it was still full of holes. He threw it to the side when he'd finished and dressed in his polyester polo shirt with some sort of logo over the pocket that he didn't recognize and a pair of trousers that were still in decent condition. There was a leather jacket in the closet that fit him, so he took it for the colder days that he knew were coming.

Returning to the bedroom, he saw Nadine curled up in the blankets. Not asleep, but just lying there with her eyes open as if she'd been thinking. "Everything okay?" he asked her.

She looked like she was going to nod, but she rolled over onto her back and just said, "Yeah."

"Are you sure?" he pressed, sitting down beside her and stroking her damp hair. It had only dried slightly in the time he'd taken for his shower.

Smiling lightly, she did nod then. "Yeah."

"What were you thinking about?"

Her lips pursed a little, but it seemed she was thinking rather than upset. "What we're going to do when we get there. Everything that happened in that hotel. Whether you're doing well enough to go back out today."

"I'm fine," he countered, hoping to stave off any further worries. "We'll figure it out. We didn't have a plan last time, and we stopped them. We can do it again."

She seemed a bit unsure, but she nodded anyway. He wished he could have sounded a lot more confident, but maybe he never sounded that way (or at least not as often as he thought). "What about the hotel? How can I stop thinking about that?" she asked then.

"I'm not sure," he admitted. "It might take time. But we'll be fine."

"I'm glad you think so. You didn't seem to think so a few days ago."

"I know. I just lost my head." He tried to think back to a time before the cyborgs ever appeared, but then he remembered that they had disguised themselves as human before, and they had been there for a long time. Was there even a time he could recall when there might not have been cyborgs anywhere? "I hope I didn't scare you with that. I couldn't help feeling it was my mistake that killed them."

"You aren't the only person who makes mistakes," she reminded him.

"True," he agreed, somewhat half-heartedly.

"Do you think you can ride your bike to the next town?" came her next question.

He tried to imagine it, tried to picture himself on the uncomfortable seat for hours on end. "Yeah," he lied. "I can do it." But he wasn't anxious to get there anyway. Would the spacecraft still be where they'd last seen it? If it wasn't there, they'd wasted a trip, and their likelihood of finding another opportunity was very low. So, he knew they had to hurry, and he couldn't afford the luxury of a few days' rest, no matter how exhausted he was.

She didn't look quite like she believed him, but she didn't argue. "Are you hungry?" she asked instead.

"Yeah," he answered, realizing suddenly how hungry he was after two days.

Sitting up, she went into the small kitchen and retrieved some oranges that had somehow miraculously appeared.

"Where did you get those?" he wanted to know.

"There was a tree not far from here. I went down when you were sleeping." She looked sheepish, as if she knew what he was going to say.

"You know you shouldn't go anywhere alone," he chided her.

She shrugged. "I won't do it again, then. Eat." Handing him one of the pieces of fruit, she kept the other and peeled it with her fingers.

He tried to do the same, but his fingernails wouldn't penetrate the skin. Finally, she took it from him and peeled it before handing it back. Taking the first bite, he thought it was the most delicious orange he'd ever eaten in his life. Never could he have imagined a piece of fruit tasting so sweet and tangy. The juices ran over his hands and chin as he couldn't keep himself from stuffing it into his mouth. She handed him a towel to clean his hands when he'd finished it, and he grinned at her. "Okay, I'm glad you found that tree," he said.

"I have a few more. We can take them with us," she told him.

He thought she might just be the wisest person he knew. "Great. You're amazing, you know?"

She smiled, blushing slightly. "Wait until you see what's for dinner."

———

They rode their bikes as far as they could, past one town and then on to the next one. If they were lucky, they would find the spaceship the next day, having cut across to take the shortest route rather than trying to throw off any pursuers. The way was narrow, only a two-lane road, and they had to ride single-file part of the way due to obstacles that made it even narrower. Sinkholes and rockslides appeared frequently.

When they reached the town, Jackson was sure he could sense some sort of electrical energy, as if the spaceship were calling to him somehow. He knew it was probably all in his head, but the nearness of it was disturbing, knowing he might be risking his life the next day. Even worse, that was the best-case scenario because if the ship was gone, they stood no chance at all of stopping the cyborgs. Their only hope was to find something to use as a weapon and to damage or destroy the beacon.

Again, they tried to find someplace to stay the night, worried now that they were too close to the cyborgs for safety. Now, Jackson wished they'd stopped in the previous town. However, he also knew that it would be better not to be too exhausted if they had to do any fighting or running the next day. So, being well-rested was imperative. The building they chose was a bank, again with a small apartment above it. There were no windows on the lower floor, only some glass doors that were easy to block off. The apartment was accessible behind the bank via a corridor that led to a couple of other offices on that level and stairs that led up to the second floor. They left their bikes in the bank but brought their overnight bags with them up to the apartment. Jackson searched the rooms: two bedrooms, one bathroom, and a main room with a kitchenette. They used the furniture from one of the bedrooms to block the windows and then pushed the sofa in front of the door. The sofa was a bulky leather item, so it required both of them to move it.

Collapsing onto a recliner in the corner, Jackson opened his overnight bag and showed Nadine the jeweler's sketchbook he'd found in the previous apartment. Jewelry designs were drawn out in detail on the pages. "Anything here you like?" he asked.

Fascinated, she took it from him and flipped through the book. "I don't know. They're all beautiful, but maybe you should design something," she suggested, handing the book back to him.

Standing, he searched the apartment until he found a pencil he could use. Then, he began sketching various simple bands that he hoped would be adequate to show her how much he loved her. He was so swept up in the task that he didn't hear her stir, and she surprised him by handing him a plate with some of the last of the salted fish and a few cherries in a small bowl to one side.

"Cherries?" he exclaimed.

She only grinned at him.

"I can't believe you found cherries!" He popped one of them into his mouth and slowly chewed the fruit off the pit.

She sat on the sofa across from him, neatly holding one of the cherries in her fingers and using her teeth to help her peel the fruit off the pit before eating it. She handed him a towel from the kitchen while she continued to eat the dessert first. "This reminds me of my first day in Paris. There was a small store down the street from my hotel with a basket of cherries in the front window. They were so sweet."

He savored each bite. "I think these are the best cherries I've ever had."

She laughed. "I doubt that, but they are very good."

"Some of it is the company I'm keeping, I'm sure," he said.

She gave him a look that suggested she was sure he was exaggerating, but she humored him anyway.

He smiled at her, sure he loved her more at that moment than he had even realized before. Yes, he did want to marry her, and she deserved something more than he could give her. However, he had inspiration for the ring, but he only wished he could make it out of gold.

———

CHAPTER
THIRTEEN

The next morning, he very reluctantly removed himself from Nadine's arms and made his way to the bathroom. He took care of basic hygiene before he searched through all of his belongings and organized his weapons. The guns may have had no effect on the beacon, but he hoped they would provide some defense against the cyborgs themselves.

Nadine sat up in the bed looking groggy, but she joined him shortly, having become just as proficient or more in the handling of weapons as he had. Once she seemed satisfied with the weapons, she left him again. This time, she brought the oranges sliced in a bowl and handed him a towel before he'd even had a chance to make a mess or ask for one. He peeled the slices and ate them hungrily. It might be his last meal *ever*, he thought, so he wanted to enjoy it. But all he could think about was the upcoming siege of the spaceship as he thought of it. He didn't want anything to happen to Nadine, but he knew he couldn't go in alone. She was the better shot of the two of them. Of course, he had every confidence that she could take care of herself, as she had proved that to him. But now that he had *plans*, he didn't want to chance losing her. Or himself, for that matter.

Before he armed himself, he gave Nadine a quick peck on the cheek for luck, but she gave him a more passionate kiss on his lips in return as if she were already aware of what he'd been thinking. She wouldn't let him down, he knew. They descended the stairs into the corridor and then entered the bank, casting the light beams around to be sure they were still alone. Then, they reclaimed their bikes and left the town, heading toward the clearing where they'd seen the strange ship. They didn't talk, afraid there would be cyborgs or collaborators nearby to hear them.

When Jackson knew they were near, he signaled to Nadine that it was up ahead. Vibrations seemed to shimmer through the air, the ground rumbling as if an earth tremor were imminent. Through the trees, he could see the reflective silver surface of the ship, but he couldn't make out any cyborgs in the vicinity. Unfortunately, he knew that didn't mean they weren't nearby, only that they weren't in the open. Fearing what might be inside the ship, he slid from the bike's seat and stealthily walked toward the clearing. He knew Nadine would back him up, knew she knew what to do. She would walk the perimeter and fire her weapon at the first sign of danger. They'd discussed it the night before, but there was only so much they could plan without knowing what they might encounter.

He crept closer and closer, taking cover behind trees as he approached and then taking a few more steps until he was almost right in front of the ship. It was larger than he remembered, about the size of a large airliner without wings. How so many of the cyborgs had squeezed inside it, he didn't know. Maybe they didn't require comfort and only packed themselves in as tightly as they could fit.

When he reached what the thought was the door, as it was the only thing that resembled an opening, with parallel vertical cracks reaching up from the ground about three and a half feet apart, he pressed his hand to the metal and waited. Nothing happened. A panel to the right of one of the cracks seemed to glow of its own volition as if it were alive, and Jackson had angered it. With no other ideas, he placed his palm on the panel, waiting while it luminesced and then, distressingly, an alarm sounded.

Terrified, he fired his assault weapon at the white-hot panel, then watched with satisfaction as the door panel slid aside. Knowing he had no choice but to proceed, he carefully swung the light beam around the spacecraft's interior, which seemed strangely empty, as the dome over the lake had been. He climbed inside, then began searching for anything he could take away with him, anything small enough to handle. He didn't even try to figure out if it was a weapon or not, as he knew he had no time.

Slipping various items into the tote bag he'd brought with him from the apartment, he hoped something in there would be of use. But without knowing any object's purpose, he simply cleaned out any storage compartments he came across. There were surprisingly few items for the number of cyborgs they'd observed, but then he remembered they could shoot vaporization beams from their hands. They had no need for any separate weapons. Would anything he'd found be of any use? He wasn't sure, but he had to hurry.

Hearing shots fired outside the ship, he leapt from the craft and searched for Nadine. He couldn't see her, but he followed the plan and sprinted for his bike. The bag of objects was slung across his shoulder, and he nearly skidded to a stop as he saw a line of cyborgs approaching ahead of him. His only choice was to escape, and for that, he needed the bike. He accelerated until he reached his transportation, then he mounted the bike and sped away, the bike bouncing over the rough ground. Without the trailer attached to it, which had been left behind at the bank, the bike traveled at a much higher speed. But where was Nadine? He looked for her at their planned rendezvous point, but her bike was nowhere to be seen.

Then, knowing she would want him to, he sped away from the clearing, heading back toward the town and a possible trap. The cyborgs would follow him, and he would be leading them directly to their hiding place. Then, out of nowhere, a figure plummeted toward him from out of the trees. His weapon raised as he rode. He almost fired at it before recognizing his fiancée. Not commenting on her sudden appearance, he simply rode along beside her, fearing that they would end up with nowhere to hide and no supplies if they didn't go back to the bank.

The cyborgs stalked briskly behind them, possibly a hundred of them. They lined the road and trailed off into the trees, blocking any escape in that direction. But they were slowly closing the distance, slowly coming up behind their prey. The sound of their metallic legs striking the road was deafening, and it struck fear in Jackson and Nadine as they struggled to stay ahead.

When he saw the bank, he headed straight for it, even as he wondered how they would be able to escape if they were surrounded. They rode their bikes through the front door but had no time to build a barricade. Jackson rode straight for the back of the building, then led Nadine into the vault, the heavy steel door slamming shut behind them as he flipped the lever for the deadbolt. Shoving a chair under the door handle and then bracing it with the table, he hoped to keep the door closed.

Even through the thick steel, they could hear the cyborgs enter the bank, could hear them stomping around and searching. But they would figure it out. Jackson didn't know how much oxygen they had in the vault, but he hoped it was enough for at least a day. Any longer than that, and he and Nadine might have to use their last-resort option, or they would suffocate to death anyway.

Suddenly the door handle moved, and the barricade shifted as if it might give way, but it somehow held. Jackson felt his breathing speed up, hoping the cyborgs wouldn't find a key or some other way to release the lock. But through the noise on the other side of the door, the searching and pacing and stomping, he heard something else. They were taking up positions. Slowly, the pacing grew silent, but he wasn't fooled into thinking the cyborgs had gone. They were waiting.

From wide eyes and panicked scrambling, Jackson and Nadine settled against the door, hoping to keep the barricade from shifting. As his adrenaline levels dropped, he almost felt like he would fall asleep, but sleep was impossible. They could die at any moment. His arms wrapped around his fiancée. He simply held her and tried to comfort her without words. The cyborgs had seen them enter the bank. They knew they were in there and were hiding. There was nowhere else to go but the vault. However, for some reason, he wasn't quite conscious of, he didn't want to make any sounds. The cyborgs couldn't be surer he and Nadine were there, but he somehow felt they would be in greater danger than already if they advertised their presence.

Nadine was no longer trembling beside him as if she had already accepted their fate, whatever that should be. Jackson hadn't quite accepted it, however, and his mind fought for alternatives and tried to think of a way out. Hours must have passed, but he lost all sense of time, and he thought it must have been half a day. He felt hungry suddenly, but their food stores were locked in their trailers, and he knew he couldn't get to them. But the food wasn't the real problem. They could go a while without food. They couldn't go long without water. Which would be the greater danger, however? Would it be the loss of oxygen, or would it be thirst which threatened them first? Which would force them to leave the vault or take fate into their own hands?

More time passed. He waited and waited. His mouth felt dry, either from thirst or fear, he wasn't sure. But he desperately wanted water. The air in the vault felt still, and the temperature was warmer than in the rest of the building without any real air circulation. He felt beads of sweat on his forehead and forming on his arms, where Nadine curled up into his side. There was also a stale smell as if all of the items left behind in the vault were susceptible to humidity and heat. He could even smell his clothes, a smell like a gym locker room. It was unpleasant, but he couldn't do anything about it.

Then, several more hours later, he could feel himself becoming lightheaded. Breathing was more difficult like layers of fabric were between himself and the oxygen. The air felt heavy and thick, and he couldn't seem to get enough of it into his lungs. I'm going to die here, he thought. But was that so bad? It was better than being torn apart by the cyborgs, wasn't it? All he had to do was go to sleep, and it would all be over. He looked down at Nadine, already asleep, and he worried that it was too late, that he would lose her and be completely alone. Barely able to face the thought, he lay there, thinking about the things he never got to do with his life.

He'd wanted a gallery show in New York, an exhibition of his photographs. Not only had he been taking photos his whole life until that point, but he'd also always hoped to do more. But had he done anything toward making that dream come true? Had he sent his portfolio to galleries, hoping for that one "yes" that would change everything? Had he worked on his resume, exhibiting his work in galleries in Smithton Lake or even Moorston Park, where he had lived? He'd done nothing at all. His dreams were only that. So, why was it so hard to believe that he would never get his simple wedding in the moonlight, making vows to Nadine? Because he never had anything work out the way he'd wanted it to, or because he hadn't tried? But this time, he *had*. He'd *tried* to kill the cyborgs. His ideas were bad ones, but he'd tried. Now, they were trapped and dying, and he would never know what it was like to be married to Nadine.

Part of him wanted to weep for his lost opportunities, but he hardly had the energy. He just sat there, struggling for air and seeing stars bloom before his eyes. Then, he was dreaming. He saw Nadine smiling at him, dressed in a gauzy white gown, a crown of flowers in her hair. The moonlight shone down on her, illuminating her in its cool blue hue. She held a small bouquet of wildflowers, and she reached out her hand…

The sound that woke him was nothing like he would have dreamed. It was an artificial, mechanical squealing sound, almost like a howl. It sounded loudly in the bank lobby, and then there was a struggle, a sound like the cyborgs were running, and then they slowly grew silent. More sounds like the squealing, more running cyborgs, more metallic pounding as they frantically left the bank. Jackson knew he had to look. He had to be sure what was happening.

Gently pushing Nadine aside, where she stirred slightly, he moved the table and then the chair. Then, he flipped the deadbolt lever over, opening the door only a crack to see out. The cyborgs were lying inactive on the floor, several dozens of them. At first, he didn't know what to make of it. Were they just rebooting after some sort of attack? Were they in some sort of sleep mode from waiting? What had happened? Confused, he opened the door slightly wider, peeking his head out to see further into the building. He tiptoed from his hiding place until he could see the lobby, where dozens more of the cyborgs lay on the floor, the lights gone from their eyes.

However, he could remember another cyborg that had looked dead and had rebooted, so he didn't feel comfortable. He ran back to the vault, shaking Nadine awake. "We have to get out of here," he whispered. "Wake up."

She sat up, looking woozy, but she stood when he helped her, and they hurried to gather their survival supplies from upstairs in the apartment, bringing down their overnight bags, which had been packed earlier in the morning. Then, they hurried to put the bags in the trailers and hitch them to the back of their bikes before pedaling out of the bank through the front door, completely in awe at the still bodies of the cyborgs, which were lying haphazardly on the ground outside. The sun was beginning to rise.

They only knew they had to get away. Jackson still felt lightheaded, but he took several deep breaths as he rode, looking back over his shoulder to be sure Nadine was with him. She kept up, but she looked unsteady, and he worried where they would be able to rest and recuperate. But what had happened to the cyborgs? There was a trail of them leading in one direction, and he wanted to follow it, to solve the mystery of what had stopped them or rendered them inactive. Whatever it was, could it be the answer to their problems?

"Wait here," he told Nadine, then he took his bike and followed the cyborg corpses, following the trail left by something more powerful than they were. But was it benevolent? The trail led around into the town and then behind a large supermarket. There, he could see what had happened. It wasn't a being more powerful than the cyborgs at all. It was the collaborator. His hand still gripped a weapon of some sort, but it had been ripped from his arm, and the arm from the torso, and so on, until the man was only small pieces, barely discernable as a human being. But Jackson recognized the man's face from the head that lay several feet away, the mouth still twisted in fear and agony. Quickly grasping the weapon from the dismembered hand, he hurriedly returned to his bike and climbed on.

Unfortunately, there were two cyborgs still standing. They turned to face him, and he raced away on his bike, almost colliding with Nadine as he retreated. "No, go, go, go!" he shouted, and they both sped off down the road and onto the highway, where they eventually realized they were not being pursued. But Jackson couldn't forget the man who'd risked his life to save them, even after he had said he couldn't. Had he had a change of heart? Had he realized Jackson was telling the truth? Or had he simply stolen a weapon and hoped to destroy the cyborgs holding him captive? Perhaps Jackson would never know, but he felt sorrow. No one deserved a death like that one. No one.

———

Turning the weapon over and over in his hand, he tried to determine how to use it. It was a rounded blob, as far as he could tell. He didn't want to accidentally fire it at himself, so he tried to tell where the "front" was and where the trigger might be if there was such a thing. Then, he held it the way he thought the hand he'd recovered it from had been holding it, trying to see if there were some way to activate it in that position. Nadine stood several feet away behind him, so he hoped she was safe. He aimed at a tree and then winced as his finger pressed into an indentation on the metal and a beam of light shot from the weapon, vaporizing the tree. Then, he almost wished he hadn't fired it at a living thing. The tree was now gone forever.

Next, he sifted through the items he'd stolen from the cyborgs' spaceship and found that one of them was an object identical to the weapon he held in his hand. So, they had a way to stop the cyborgs after all, but only a few of them at a time, or would the weapon vaporize the beacon the way it had vaporized the tree? He hoped it would at least disable it. "Did you want this?" he asked Nadine, holding out the second weapon.

She took it gingerly from him as if afraid of activating it accidentally. Then, she copied his grip and fired it at a boulder, watching with fear and satisfaction as the thing disappeared from the roadway.

"Okay, just be careful with it," he told her unnecessarily. Then, he put the metallic blob, about the size of a small mandarin, in the tote bag with the other technological samples he'd stolen. "We'll figure out what these other things do later. Let's find a place to stop."

Riding on, they approached another town, but they debated continuing and stopping at the cottage before heading to confront the cyborgs again. In the end, they decided it was a needless risk, that they might end up losing the cottage if they chanced staying there for even one night. If the cyborgs won, they would be fleeing again anyway. They rode around the small town, which had only one main street and a few short cross streets that led nowhere.

Most of the buildings had only one story, but there were a couple of hotels, and Jackson picked the most secure of the two, one that had three stories and a red brick façade, with no windows on the first floor and only the two doors. The front door was a sturdy wooden door with a brass handle. He opened it and went inside with his flashlight, checking the rooms carefully before they barricaded the front and back doors, then climbed upstairs. Everything seemed outdated. The wallpaper was dark green, and the carpet was peeling off the floor. It wouldn't be comfortable, but they had few choices.

They blocked the window with one of the mattresses by pushing it up and leaning it against the blackout curtains, then they used the light to prepare a small meal. It used almost the last of their food stores, but they wouldn't be out much longer anyway. If they succeeded in destroying the cyborgs, they would go home to their cottage and garden and start over. If they failed, they would be dead anyway.

They each had one orange apiece to eat for breakfast

the next morning, but they ate the last of the cherries for dessert, thinking they deserved it after such an awful day. It felt like his last request before dying. But then again, maybe that was the orange he'd have the next day. The cherries were an odd luxury after the bank and having nearly suffocated. It felt hollow and extravagant at the same time like it wasn't enough, but it was somehow more than he could comprehend at that moment.

"Do you think we can plant a cherry tree?" Nadine asked him, licking the fruit juices off her fingers.

The question seemed out of place amid his depressing thoughts. He couldn't forget the collaborator's disassembled body, the images stuck on replay. Nadine had seen it before, but he knew she wasn't immune. She was probably having flashbacks and trying to distract herself before her own thoughts became far too dark. "Yeah. Why not? We might need a bigger lot, though. Ours is pretty small," he replied, trying to keep his tone light.

"We can tear down the house next door," she suggested, setting aside her plate and staring at him for his reaction.

"Yeah, that wouldn't be too difficult. We might as well build a larger house, too. Why don't we tear down three or four houses to make room? That way, we'll have more bedrooms, and we can have room for more fruit trees."

Her eyes stared at his, looking completely unsure whether she thought he was joking. Then, she suddenly broke down in a fit of giggles. He laughed finally, thinking it felt good to have a light moment after everything had been so dismal.

"Okay, so let's tear down the whole block. We'll build

a castle there with a moat and everything." He grinned, and she rolled over onto the floor, still giggling. "You don't like my idea," he insisted, still teasing.

"If you want to build it, I will say it's fine," she deadpanned. "But you'll have to clean it, too."

He pursed his lips, faking deep thought. "Never mind. It wasn't such a good idea after all."

She laughed even harder, and he shushed her quietly, still trying to keep from making too much noise. Grinning, she shook her head as she began cleaning up the dishes. Even he couldn't help smiling as he helped her pour the trash into the receptacle and then to rinse the plates and bowls they'd used before replacing them in their bags.

"Okay, let's get some sleep," he said reluctantly. He slid underneath the blankets, which were in about the same condition as the rest of the room. It was understandable after five years, but still disgusting. Nadine climbed in next to him and draped an arm over his chest so she could rest her head on his shoulder. One more night. It would be settled the next day, one way or another.

———

CHAPTER
FOURTEEN

When he woke, he wasn't sure if it was still night or whether morning had arrived. However, he didn't feel strongly enough about getting out of the bed to check. He dreaded the rest of the journey and the possible negative outcome. Nadine yawned and stretched her arms, and then she slipped from the bed and stumbled into the bathroom. He sighed but stood and retrieved the oranges from Nadine's bag. Then, he took the time to slice them and put them in bowls while she finished rinsing herself in the shower. When she returned to the bedroom, he was sitting on one of the chairs eating, so she joined him at the small table, thanking him for preparing their meager breakfast. He knew it wasn't enough, but they had nothing else. Everything else was at home, which he hoped they would see later that day.

Even Nadine seemed introspective and not her bubbly self that he'd become used to. He understood. It wasn't as if he felt like himself either. They quietly washed the dishes and put them away, then without talking about it, they packed and went downstairs to the bikes they'd left in the lobby. This is it, he thought to himself, pedaling out of the building and into the street. When they reached the highway, it was a two-lane road lined with lots of short, stubby trees as they neared the coast. There were only a few miles until they reached the ridge and the clearing where they'd seen the cyborgs setting up what he had assumed was a beacon, and he worried that the weapons they had were not enough. However, the cyborgs' own technology was more likely to be effective than anything Jackson or Nadine had previously.

He watched the scenery change as they traveled, watching for the low hills that would signal they'd moved out of the mountains. The road led to the original highway they'd taken to flee the area several days or weeks before. When they reached it, the familiar feel of the landscape struck Jackson like a physical blow, as he hadn't realized how much he'd missed his home. Of course, it felt more like a home with Nadine, and he wanted to start a new chapter with her as his wife. He hoped it wasn't futile to dream of it, to dream of a life full of peace and love.

Slowly, the mountains gave way to hills, and then the hills slowly gave way to low dunes. There was tall grass and a few scrubby trees all around, and they both headed across the field to the ridge that seemed almost foreign in the daylight. He worried about being spotted and signaled to Nadine to wait. They dropped off their bikes and crouched down below the rise, waiting. Even as the sun began to set early, with winter nearing, they waited what felt like hours before the sky turned from flaming orange to rosy mauve and then to dark navy scattered with stars. They didn't dare use the light, but the stars were enough to illuminate their way as they climbed the ridge and knelt below the tree line.

They knew the cyborgs were still there by the glow from the other side of the hill, the lights so bright in the darkness that it was almost like day. There were about two dozen cyborgs still in the vicinity, scattered around the clearing and carrying various devices, including the beacon-like cone they'd seen before. The ship was still there, the one about the size of a biplane, sitting a few yards from the beacon, and Jackson worried there were more cyborgs inside. If they fired the alien weapons and they had no effect, they probably would not be able to escape quickly enough. It was enough to make him pause, and he tried desperately to gather enough courage to act.

He watched Nadine for a cue or some sort of sign that she was going to do something, but she seemed to be monitoring the activity below them as if she might be able to tell what the cyborgs were trying to do. The beacon must have been functioning at that point because they seemed to ignore it completely. Instead, the cyborgs were setting up several objects that looked like pointed stanchions with lighted tips in a circle around the clearing. The stanchions had stands that the cyborgs were assembling and then placing at the bases of the long, sharpened rods that formed the shafts. Then, they took them to the next location in the circle and dug them into the ground, leaving the shafts protruding from the loose soil.

Whatever they were doing, Jackson knew it wasn't anything that would benefit any of the remaining humans. He knew it was bad, that it would bring more cyborgs to Earth somehow. Not taking the time to wonder what purpose any of it served, he wanted to destroy all of it, hoping the cyborgs would never return. But how close did they need to get? He took a deep breath, steadying his nerves. Then, he waved a hand at Nadine to get her attention. However, right at that moment, he heard a mechanical roaring sound, like an alarm was triggered. When he looked up, he saw that the cyborgs were standing still, facing him, with their arms extending out toward him almost accusingly.

Remembering the tree that had disappeared from his path after one of the cyborgs shot a beam of light from its palm, he feared he was dead. The rounded weapon was in his hand, but he wasn't sure he could fire it quickly enough. He dodged, crying out as debris struck his arms, legs, and face as it flew up from where he'd just been kneeling. Terrified, he looked to where Nadine had been, and she was curled in a ball as if she'd been hit and had rolled down the hill partway.

Anger boiled up in him. Fear for Nadine nearly exploded out of him as he shouted a primal scream, and then he stood at the top of the ridge and aimed. Several cyborgs collapsed as the light beam struck them, although they didn't disappear like the other objects they'd destroyed, he ducked as another beam of light shot toward him from off to his right. The tree next to him luminesced and vanished, and he rolled to one side and fired his weapon again. Several more of the cyborgs toppled over, and he ran down into the clearing, ripping the stanchions from their positions as he neared the beacon. Barely able to contain his fury, he fired the weapon again and again. When he reached the beacon, he aimed and then saw the lights on the beacon go out. Unsure whether it was still functioning, he wanted to fire again, but the cyborgs were advancing on him. There were still six of them left, and they very nearly surrounded him.

He wasn't sure he would make it out then. Why had he run down into the midst of them when the weapon worked at a distance? It had only been that he wasn't thinking, wasn't concentrating at all. He'd only *felt*. Pain and despair filled him as he thought of Nadine lying unconscious or dead on the hillside, and he worried that if he died there, she would never know what happened to him. What if she woke, and he'd been vaporized, and she never saw him again?

Thinking of the ache she would feel, the emptiness at not being sure, he felt the anger flare in him again. He couldn't let them do this to her. Surrounded completely now, he ran toward the ship, hoping for shelter. Firing the weapon over his shoulder, his aim was mostly wide, and he missed, striking the ground only a few feet away from each of them. The ship's door was open, and he leapt for it, his hands gripping the opening and then pulling himself inside. The interior lit up, glowing as if the materials themselves were alive. However, it was empty of other beings, and he started to slam the door shut before he thought he saw something moving on the ridgeline.

Standing in the doorway, he continued firing, and he hit two of the remaining cyborgs at last, leaving only four, which advanced ever closer, only yards away now. But the figure he'd seen streaked across the clearing, rounding the last of the stanchions, and then came nearer and nearer until he could see that he was saved. Nadine fired a few beams from her weapon out toward the last cyborgs as she ran. He stepped aside as she leapt into the ship beside him, then he shoved the door into place, hearing a *thunk* as it sealed. Metallic squeals sounded on the hull as some sort of weapons fire struck the ship, but Jackson stood and searched around what he guessed was the front. A protrusion erupted from the floor near what looked almost like a viewscreen, except it was dark and nonfunctioning. Waving his hand in front of it, he hoped he could figure out where he was facing, hoping the ship had weapons of its own.

The screen remained dark, and frustrated, he slapped his hand repeatedly on all surfaces, remembering the control center and how glyphs had appeared in the air. That happened now, and he wished he could read the language.

The alien symbols were rounded and glowed white in the air, appearing almost solid and tactile. When he touched the largest one at Nadine's prompting, the entire ship interior made a beeping noise, and the screens came on. Encouraged, he sat on the chair-like protrusion and gestured to Nadine, who tightly gripped the back of the seat. Then, as new symbols and controls appeared in the air in front of him, he tried to figure out how to aim. Putting his hand around one of the new controls, a bar that appeared out of the air, he turned the lever until he could feel the entire ship moving, rotating, and then he pressed a button. Hoping it activated the weapons, he could see on the viewscreen that the remaining four cyborgs had fled the clearing. They didn't run. They only walked purposefully away. But the ground erupted around them, and Jackson continued firing until he saw the beacon in the center of the clearing blast apart.

The four cyborgs stiffened as if struck by lightning, then they tumbled to the earth, falling over where they stood, the lights dying from their eyes. Unsure if it were only the cyborgs near the beacon that were disabled, Jackson wanted to patrol the area. However, he knew he could barely operate the ship, and it would take time to learn to do so properly.

He and Nadine discussed the controls, trying out various movements and combinations over the next few hours until they could get the ship into the air. They flew low over the trees, hoping any other cyborgs would think it was their own. But when they reached the location of the other ship, the cyborgs that had surrounded it were completely inert, lying motionless on the ground as if they'd dropped while walking. Jackson fired the ship's weapons anyway. The cyborgs dissolved into nothing as the light struck them. He was sure he'd missed a few of them, but the threat was greatly reduced with most of them gone.

Over the next several hours, they repeated the maneuvers, circling the sky for any signs that there were any more cyborgs around. However, it was obvious that they were deactivated and gone, that there had been fewer of them this time. They found a few more of the alien ships over the next few days as they searched the countryside near their home and on the far side of the world, as the ship they'd commandeered traveled at great speeds, and they took great satisfaction in blasting the alien technology into oblivion and watching it vanish from the Earth forever. Relieved one day when they found no more, Jackson landed the ship in the clearing in the trees near the house and buried it under debris to keep it hidden. In the event that the cyborgs ever returned, he knew how to use the technology now. He could fight them off if he had to. It was finally over. At last, they could live the peaceful life they'd dreamed of.

———

One clear night a month later and under a full moon, Jackson led Nadine out to the windswept beach. The stars glittered like jewels, reflecting in the waves that crashed on the shore and causing them to glow and shimmer as if millions of fireflies were greeting them beneath. Her hair was whipped by the breeze. She'd pulled it back with a ribbon and tied it with white blossoms. She was dressed in a billowing white lace gown that she'd found in a shop in the town, and he wore a white tuxedo with a navy-blue tie. A small bouquet of white and periwinkle wildflowers was clutched in her hands,

which shook slightly, but she smiled warmly when she saw
the wide ring of candles flickering on the sands. He led her to
the center, then he took her hands in his.

"Nadine Dardenne, I promise to love you forever, as
you are and as who you are yet to be. I promise to be patient
with you and to listen to your advice. I promise to remember
that all we create between us will be filled with love. I promise
to help you discover and achieve your dreams. I promise to
share my heart and soul with you, no matter how difficult
things shall become. I promise to love you completely and
loyally as long as I shall live." He took her left hand and slid a
ring of carved abalone shell onto her finger. The floral pattern
swirled around the top of the ring, matching the pendant he'd
given her for her birthday.

"Jackson Riley, I choose you to be my everything. I am
overjoyed to be your wife and to share my life with you. I
vow to support you as you will support me. I will be with
you for as long as we both shall live. I will love you and only
you. I will advise you and guide you, knowing that all you
give me is rooted in love. Give me your hand today, and I will
give you forever." Smiling shyly, she took his hand, sliding a
simple band of polished abalone shell onto his finger.

Knowing it was her first attempt to make anything,
he admired the band, which was crudely carved but made
with all the affection she had for him, making it priceless. He
smiled at her, then reached down and took her into his arms,
kissing her passionately. "You are mine, and I am yours," he
said into her ear. She repeated the words, and he held her,
feeling he never wanted the night to end. "You are mine, and
I am yours," he said again. They sank to the sand, where he

reached into his pocket and handed her a small, wrapped box. "This is for you."

She grinned childishly as she slit open the paper, putting it aside and watching the wind take it away. Inside the paper was a tiny wooden box that he'd obviously made himself, which held a small pit on a handmade cushion. "What is this?" she asked.

"It's a cherry tree. It's a bit small now, but it will grow with all the love you will give to it."

"I love it! Thank you!" she exclaimed, carefully shielding the pit from the breeze and closing up the box, even as she took a moment to hold it and fight back the tears of happiness. Gathering herself, she said, "This is for you." And she stood, walking over to a nearby copse of palm trees and sliding a large package over to set it in front of him.

His gaze was quizzical as he took the cloth wrapping and untied the ribbon binding it, revealing a small weaving loom and a drop spindle. "You got me a weaving loom?" he asked.

"Yes. And a drop spindle. I hope you understand—"

"These are the best gifts I could have ever gotten. Thank you," he told her honestly.

Her expression showed enormous relief as if she might have been afraid that he would have been offended. Instead, she grinned at him, taking his hand and leading him back to the house, where several more candles had been lit, setting the windows aglow with their warm light.

END

ACKNOWLEDGMENTS

Although this book was immensely fun to write, I have several people to thank for helping it come together.

First, I have to thank Hermione Lee for providing valuable insight into the manuscript and helping me create something more than just a story about two people encountering a familiar threat. I also have her to thank for suggesting I write a sequel to *Descent of the Vile* at all, which was originally a stand-alone novel. Also, I want to thank my father, Alfredo Peña, for always being there for me. I had some health issues while writing this book, and his support was invaluable. My mother, Charlotte Peña, always helps me to look beyond writing and publishing, and I couldn't do this without our frequent coffee breaks. Thank you! Heather Dixon, as always, provided insight on the potential covers and had to endure my endless text messages on the subject. Thanks for getting sushi with me, too! Thank you, as always, to Inge Pratt, who was the person who suggested I try to publish my first novella. I am still writing because of her support and enthusiasm. Karen Fuller always helps my manuscripts become more than just a few words thrown together. I couldn't do this without her editing skills, as I make more mistakes than I would like to admit. Lastly, I have to thank everyone at World Castle Publishing. You create such beautiful books, and I am very grateful to you for everything you do. Thank you!

ABOUT THE AUTHOR

Cheryl Peña was born in San Antonio, Texas, to multiracial parents and grew up with an interest in art and literature. Before she was able to read, she was writing books in one way or another. By age ten, she had reached college-level language skills and won first place in the National Language Arts Olympiad when she was eleven years old. She graduated with an honors BFA in photography and worked as a professional photographer for a couple of years before eventually settling in the legal field. Upon the death of her twin sister in 2014, she decided to write professionally in her sister's honor. She is the author of the thriller novella *The House of Wynne Lift*, as well as the science-fiction *Descent of the Vile* duology.